Tyson Anthony Presents
Naked

1 - Exposed

Tye knew what it felt like to feel naked and exposed. Everybody downstairs at his father's New Year's party knew Tye slept with men. Tye didn't mind them knowing, not ashamed of his sexuality. But the issue was that it hurt his father's reputation and the man's entire career as a counselor. It was discovered that Tye was sleeping with one of the young men his father was tasked with mentoring out of the streets and into a better life. Tonight this party was all about restoring his father's reputation. And Tye would soon have to join them all downstairs, all the people he was exposed too.

Tye stood in the bathroom, fresh out of a shower, staring at himself in his bathroom mirror. His mocha skin was still damp, droplets of water slowly making its way down his toned body to the bathroom floor. Most of his father's friends and colleagues once knew Tye as mister innocent who kept all of his focus on college, helped out around the community, and his clean cut appearance mirror that image.

Tye was tattoo free, piercing free, kept his buzzcut hair trimmed, and had a big smile that could convince anybody he was nothing but innocent. But they all now knew a different Tye. The Tye who's nude photos that were sent through a private text ended up all over Facebook. He learned his lesson, don't fuck his father's clients, especially the vengeful ones who couldn't handle being dumped. And now he had to convince a room full of people that he'd changed his ways. Tye exhaled heavily and stepped from his bathroom.

He got dressed, slipping on some dark jeans, a white polo shirt, and some all red sneakers. Tye did his best to deliver business casual by deciding not to wear a hat, though he was sure anything that wasn't a suit and tie would disappoint his father. He checked his phone to see if his mother had called him. The woman joined the Peace Corps and was now somewhere in Mexico and rarely called. Tye figured she would send him some words of encouragement like she usually did, but nothing came through. This was the one night he really could use her encouraging and soothing hippy words.

Tye stuffed his phone in his pocket and headed downstairs to a packed house. All eyes were on him even though most pretended they weren't looking his way. But things weren't as extreme as they were when the entire situation went down one year ago. Finally, they were starting to accept his father back amongst the elite of Riverbed, Connecticut. A couple of the elite showing up to the man's party was proof of that after spending the year avoiding any thing he hosted.

Tye looked across the room to spot his short, round, and bald father sucking up to the church members, politicians, and fellow professionals that once respected him so highly. These were the people that would send troubled men and women into the man's home for guidance. But after the controversy, the joke around town was that he was basically now running a brothel and Tye was the lone ho on staff.

Tye bumped into a fragile and ancient Preacher Ramsey.

Ramsey plastered on a smile and pushed up his bifocals, "Well look who joined the party."

Tye shook the man's hand, "Hey, preach."

"You got so damn big," Ramsey said as he looked Tye up and down, "How you doing?"

"I'm doing good," Tye said, "How are you?"

"I'm doing as well as the lord allows me to be," Ramsey said, "You haven't been to church since...you know."

"I've been busy," Tye said.

3

"Busy? Busy how? Because from what I heard you aren't even in college anymore," Ramsey said, "How old are you now boy?"

"I'm twenty-three," Tye said.

"You're not a boy then," Ramsey said, "You're grown man. You need to be getting your education."

"I'll go back...eventually," Tye said.

Tye had no interest in getting an education at the moment. He had plans to go back someday and follow in his father's footsteps, but for now he enjoyed being around the man and helping him by keeping up with the house and working as his part-time assistant. Tye also wanted to focus on helping the man rebuild his reputation after he destroyed it. That required Tye being in Riverbed and volunteering like crazy around town for events.

"If you ever need guidance, come talk to me," Ramsey said, "I know your dad can tell you what he learned from his books, but I can tell you what you need to learn from an even better book. The good book. Now I'm going to go get me some shrimp from the food table while my wife isn't around me watching what I eat."

"I'll holler if I see her coming," Tye said as he patted the man on his shoulder.

Tye continued working the room, interacting with the snobby upper class of Riverbed. Most of them boasted about their careers, charitable acts, and extravagant homes. Others were not shy about grilling Tye and talked about his sexuality as if it was some sort of disease. Not everybody at the New Year's party were a part of the upper class. Riverbed had a serious wealth gap.

Outside of the predominately black suburbs that were packed with doctors, lawyers, politicians, professors, and wealthy church goers, you had the all American ghetto. And the majority of his father's clients were from the lower class, which the man preferred since that's where his roots were embedded. In one corner of the party, a couple of the man's clients hung out looking out of place.

Tye went over and greeted them, most by name. A couple of them did their best to avoid interacting with him, aware of his sexuality while those who knew him for a bit didn't care. There were a couple of new faces, including a pregnant girl with hair pulled back in a ponytail and with tattoos on her neck. Another new client was a guy who stood the furthest to the back, who wore all black, had dreads down to his shoulders, and awkwardly sipped from a glass of champagne. Tye simply nodded at the dreaded stranger and he looked away from him. He was sure the other clients had fill the newbie in on his leaked photos scandal.

Tye continued working the room, his face starting to hurt from smiling so much. One lady forced him to dance with her and he had stopped to show another how to work her iPhone camera. She took a picture of Tye and sent it to her granddaughter who was single and looking according to the out of touch woman. Tye broke away from the awkward situation and made it over to his father Herbert who was chatting with two twin doctors who he had actually mentored during their stint in med school. Like his father, the twins also grew up in the hood of Riverbed.

Tye nodded at the twins, "Sup, Brian and Bryant."

"Man, you've grown up," Bryant said.

"Yeah, I remember when your dad used to come visit us on campus and you would be glued to your Nintendo DS," Brian added.

"I can't get any younger, but if you two find a cure for aging, hit me up," Tye joked.

The twins laughed as they walked away from the father and son.

Herbert leaned in close to Tye, "That was perfect."

"What was perfect?" Tye asked.

"The jokes, the smiles, the dancing with the old ladies," Herbert said, "I'm proud of you son. I wish you had worn a suit but I just have to take what I can get. So far you've been the super son I needed tonight. I've been working my mouth off trying to talk myself back into certain social circles. A few cops are going to start sending new clients my way again, the politicians have all promised to talk to some state officials, but the church isn't budging. I'm sure Preacher Ramsey won't mind, but his wife is homophobic as hell. Glenda wants you to burn."

"That bitch," Tye said, "I called her dress pretty tonight."

Herbert nudged him, "Don't call her that...even if she is. Have you heard from your mom?"

"Nope," Tye said.

"Do you think she's having an affair in Mexico?" Herbert asked.

"Yup," Tye said, "She looks way too happy in her Facebook pictures to be in Mexico."

Herbert scoffed, "I don't want a divorce, not now. I have to rebuild my reputation before having to go through that process. Divorcing your mother will only turn the church away from me more. And if the church really wanted to screw me over, they would start turning the politicians against me."

"Do you think I should not work as your assistant anymore?" Tye asked.

"No, no, no, you're fine," Herbert said, "I tell them it's how I keep you close so I can mentor you."

"I'm going to go finish working the room," Tye said.

"Me too," Herbert said as he tugged at his snug suit jacket, "We make a good team, right?"

"We're like Jay Z and Beyonce," Tye joked, "And with your hips, you're definitely Queen B."

Herbert smirked at his son, shook his head at him, and went to go do some more brownnosing.

Tye was far too old to be torn apart by the state of his parents' marriage. They didn't dislike each other, but simply didn't excite each other anymore. His father was more of a bookworm who only cared about work and being on top. His mother was a free spirit who liked nude beaches and feeding sick children. He came out to them both when he was sixteen. His parents used their common sense and understood that he was born gay, not turned this way by Satan like some believed. After chatting with a man who smelled like cigarettes, Tye headed out onto the back patio for some fresh air.

The stars were in the sky and the swing set he hadn't used for ages creaked as the wind blew through the backyard. Tye could remember every cookout, birthday party, and hours he spent wit his friends in this backyard. Most of his friends were now simply people who pictures he liked on Instagram and Facebook. The only friends he actually kept up with were the ones he slept with. Out on the back patio, Avery joined Tye. Avery lived next door with his wife Dr. Shelia. The lanky man, who was as smooth as his voice, was a member of a singing trio that were big back in the seventies. Now he mostly did reunion tours. Avery wore a pair of dark slacks and a blood red dress shirt, smelled like aftershave, and his wavy low cut hair glistened in the moon light.

"I think you're the freshest dude at the party," Tye said.

Avery laughed, "Thank you. What are you doing out here?"

"Taking a break from rubbing elbows," Tye said, "You?"

"I've run out of things to say," Avery said, "Usually Shelia does all the talking."

"Where is she?" Tye asked, "Wait, let me guess, the hospital?"

"As always," Avery said, "But she wanted to be here for your father. She hates how he's being treated."

"Me too," Tye said, "And I feel bad because it's all my fault."

"You didn't do anything wrong," Avery said, "You had sex. We all do. And I know you're getting more blow back because of the gay thing, but half of the men in that room probably have your pictures saved on their phones. Nobody can convince me that the twin with the birthmark on his neck...I think Bryant, isn't gay."

"If he is I need his number now," Tye joked.

"How old are you?" Avery asked as he softly laughed.

"Twenty-three, why?" Tye asked.

"The twins...they're about thirty-five," Avery said, "Bryant is a bit too old for you, right?"

"Nope," Tye said, "I don't know how you straight dudes do it, but fifty-five is my limit."

Avery took his phone and put it before Tye's face, "Well...I'm forty-five."

Tye looked at the phone as Avery scrolled through the leaked photos of him that changed so much in his life. A few photos was of Tye in bed holding his dick as he looked to a camera and others were of him on the bathroom floor, on his knees, with his booty arched. He remember waking up and seeing all of these photos on Facebook and the dreading wait for them to be removed.

Tye looked to Avery who wore a serious look on his face, "Why do you have those?"

"Because they're beautiful," Avery said as he put his phone away.

"Avery, stop playing," Tye said.

"I'm serious," Avery said, "You're beautiful as hell. And I know about two other guys in there who I drink with that think the same thing. I won't say who because I'm not the type to go telling people's business, but I'm making the choice to approach you and let you know what I think about you before one of them tries too."

"Man, I've known you since I was like...thirteen," Tye said as he awkwardly rubbed at his neck.

"And?" Avery said, "We're both men now."

"But you're married to Shelia," Tye said, "I like Shelia and I don't think she would like this convo we're having."

"But Shelia doesn't like you," Avery said, "She thinks you're selfish just like your mother. And the way you messed up things for your father, one of her closest friends, only made her dislike you even more for your selfish ways. Don't let people fool you Tye. Many times she's called you a selfish faggot."

Tye didn't want to believe none of that about Shelia, "No way."

"Yes way," Avery said, "And I've had to sit there and hold my tongue. I like your entire family, even your mother. I respect your father. And I can't stop thinking about you. I like the way you dress, talk, and you know that smile is killer, right? But seeing those pictures of you took things to a new level. I understand that I'm a married, but that's my sin to deal with on my own."

"What do you want from me?" Tye asked.

"Don't deny me," Avery said, "Let's go over to my house."

"Why?" Tye asked.

"To talk," Avery said, "To get away from this party for a bit."

"If I come you're going to have to tell me about these other men with my pictures," Tye said.

Avery rubbed at his square jaw, "I do?"

"Yeah," Tye said, "It's awkward and I'm nosey."

Avery thought about it, "No matter what, you can't say anything."

"I won't," Tye said, "Not about them, not about you. I know how being exposed feels, it's not fun."

"I'll tell you over some drinks," Avery said, "Follow me."

Avery made his way off the patio and over towards his backyard. Tye followed after the man shocked about everything he learned tonight.

2 - Pillows

Tye never figured Avery would be gay, especially because he was married and all the stories he told about the groupies he slept with in the seventies. The man even had a few kids out there from women in his past. Tye stopped being naïve, well aware that a lot of gay men were living double lives or that Avery simply could've been bisexual.

As the man arrived to the backdoor of his home, he looked back and smirked at Tye. Tye wasn't going to lie, Avery looked good for forty-five. And during his virgin teenage years, Tye would lay in bed and wonder what the man's dick looked like. He always imagined the tall man's dick hung down too his knees. Tye's big imagination about guy's dick size sometime left him disappointed.

Avery opened the back door and Tye followed him through the dark home. He led Tye to the room that he referred to as his man cave. On the walls of the burgundy painted room was past awards Avery had won. There was also a minibar, some recording equipment, and in the center of the floor was a bed of pillows that Avery always boasted about when he first got in it installed.

Avery motioned at the bed of black pillows, "Take your shoes off and relax."

"I came over here to talk," Tye said.

"I know," Avery said as he approached his minibar and poured two drinks, "Relax."

Tye kicked off his red sneakers and dropped down onto the comfy bed of pillows, "Okay, now I see why you're always talking about this bed."

Avery laughed as he kicked off his shoes and grabbed the two drinks from the bar, "Shelia thinks it's tacky."

"Do you guys have sex on this at all?" Tye asked.

"No, she's boring," Avery said, "She likes dick given to her in bed. I mostly write on these pillows."

"Oh, so what are you...gay...bi, what?" Tye asked.

Avery carefully held the drinks as he joined Tye down on the bed of pillows, "I like sex, how about that?"

"Fine, whatever," Tye asked as he reached out for his drink, "Who are the other creeps with my pictures?"

Avery passed Tye his drink, "Larry who owns the cable installation company and Isaiah."

"Wait, Isaiah as in Preacher Ramsey's pride and joy?" Tye asked, shocked.

"Yup," Avery said, "If his mother knew, she would drop dead."

"I know," Tye said, "How did you guys even connect?"

"I always knew about Larry from way back in the day," Avery said, "He used to be at every disco club high on drugs and sleeping with whoever. Unlike me, instead of getting married he just kept his life private. And as for Isaiah, I bumped into him at a sex shop years ago outside the city, carrying almost every gay DVD they had in stock. Larry is still pretty distant, but we chat. And when I'm desperate, I'll go over to Isaiah's place and we'll just watch porn and jerk off together. No sex. I have zero attraction to him."

"I used to," Tye said as he sipped his drink, "But when I was a teen I liked anybody with a dick."

Avery laughed, "Isaiah has a pretty big dick. It's uncut."

"I hate uncut dicks," Tye said as he laughed, "You killed any attraction I had left for him."

"It's a nice dick, you're too picky," Avery sipped his drink, "But apparently you like those hood boys."

"Excuse me?" Tye said before finishing off his drink.

10

"You know what I'm talking about," Avery said, "I want the full truth about this entire thing with your father's client. How did it start? What happened? And what went wrong? Because there's a million different stories around Riverbed right now."

Tye never told anybody the full story, because like Avery said, they all had their own versions. And he never told his parents, because talking about his sex life with them was something he didn't want to do. He hoped there was nobody out there in the world eager to tell their parents how much dick they could take.

"First, let me just say...that I started it," Tye admitted, "I basically baited this guy into my bed. When I first met him, I treated him just like all the other clients. But the more he came around, the more fine this dude started to look to me. And though I'm not just into hood boys, his entire fresh out of jail vibe got to me. A lot of his aggression and anger came from his pent up sexuality."

"How in the hell did you find that out?" Avery asked.

"I'm nosey," Tye said, "I read his file."

"That's not right," Avery said.

"I know, but I just wanted to know more about him," Tye said, "But anyways, my father has a very bad habit of scheduling sessions but forgetting them. And he scheduled a session with my obsession whose name was King but my dad was actually out of town. I pretended I didn't know my dad would never arrive so sat with King just chatting him up and flirting hard. Tired of the games, I just started rubbing on him and he fucked me on the couch."

"Wow," Avery said, "And what if he had punched your teeth out?"

"I was horny and so confident with my snooping that I didn't even think of that scenario," Tye said.

"So, how did you guys go from that to having yourself exposed all over Facebook?" Avery asked.

"Well, I should've read all of his file," Tye said, "He was very possessive and started threatening me and shit when I wouldn't answer his calls. There was even one time when he showed up on campus and tried to start a fight with me. I had to let him know, we were just friends with benefits. He got mad, had some pics I sent him forever ago and tadah. I'm the town ho."

Avery laughed, "You're not the town whore."

"People act like it," Tye said.

11

"I'll never forget the brothel line," Avery said, "That one really hurt your father. I can't believe they printed that about him. But even though he was hurt, as you know, I was glad to finally see what you were hiding under your clothes. As I said before, you're beautiful. And your ass...is just right, not too muscular, not too fat, just right. I'm so glad you came over tonight."

"To talk," Tye said, "I mean...were you thinking about my ass when I was thirteen?"

Avery chugged the rest of his drink and set the glass aside, "Why would you ask that shit?"

"Because I can," Tye said, "You've known me for a while...at what point did you start thinking about me sexually?"

"Honestly?" Avery asked as he got more comfortable on his bed of pillows.

"Yeah," Tye said as he cuddled up to a pillow, interested to know what about him sparked the man's lust.

"And you won't judge me?" Avery asked.

"Not at all," Tye said.

Avery smirked, "You're so nosey."

"Just tell me already," Tye said as he playfully punched Avery in the arm.

"I remember the day and all the feelings I had," Avery said as he looked to Tye, "I had just gotten off a long tour and Shelia didn't come pick me up from the airport. Instead, I took a taxi home and when the car pulled up you and some of those loud ass dudes you used to hang with were all in your dad's front lawn tossing around a football. I know for sure you were seventeen at the time because you had a car already. You were wearing some red basketball shorts and was barefoot. At that point man, your body was really on point."

"Before I packed on the freshman fifteen," Tye said, "My Instagram was off the chain back then."

Avery laughed, "But anyways. That was the first time I saw you in a sexual way. It was your ass in those shorts and that smile on your face that just had me locked in. I remember walking in the house and you didn't even notice me. Shelia was sitting on the couch acting as if she didn't know I was coming home. We argued and whatever and I came in here to cool off." Avery pointed to the lone window in his man cave, "I remember just laying down and staring out the window. And after all these years, I realized I could see into your room. Your blinds were up, which they never are."

12

Tye thought about it, "Hold up, I remember this day. My uncle was in town and was staying in my room. He used to smoke so left the window up. I never up my window because I like my room to be dark as fuck, it's more relaxing that way. Man, things were so different back then. My mom was a housewife."

"I do remember your uncle being in town," Avery said, "But anyways, I remember seeing you running into your bedroom, closing your door and then it happened. You changed out of your sweaty gyms shorts and I got a nice side view of you naked. It was only for a lil bit because you changed so quick into some clothes and rushed out. In this very spot where I am now, I jerked off to that image. Afterwards, I won't lie, I felt like a pedophile. I felt dirty, perverted, and even went online to look up the age of consent."

"You spied on me," Tye said, "But I'm not mad."

"I was mad at myself," Avery said, "And needed to cleanse myself of those feelings. So right away, I charged into the living room, forgave Shelia and ate her pussy until I felt normal. I couldn't stand living next door to you. It reached the point of me wanting to move. Shelia agreed because she didn't like your mom. But because we were both so busy, you were heading off to college before we could decide on a house."

"Do you still look up to my room?" Tye asked.

"Nah," Avery said, "It's like those blinds are glued together. You never touch them."

Tye laughed, "Any bit of light can ruin a good nap for me, man. Interesting conversation though."

"Yeah," Avery said as he checked the time on his phone, "We still have thirty minutes before midnight."

"I bet my dad is wondering where I am," Tye said, "I don't feel like going back over there."

"Then stay here," Avery said, "We can talk some more."

"And what if your wife comes home and finds us laying in here together?" Tye said.

"We're just laying down," Avery said.

"You and the town ho," Tye said.

"Well, the door is locked," Avery said, "So you can just hop out the window if she shows up."

"Why did you lock the door?" Tye asked with a smirk.

"It's a habit," Avery said, "I don't like her barging in here."

"Because you might be jerking off to my pictures," Tye said, "Delete them."

"Why?"

"Because it's creepy," Tye said.

Avery took out his phone, "I'll delete them if you take off your clothes now."

"No deal," Tye said.

"I'll delete them if you strip down to your underwear then," Avery said.

Tye thought about it, "I want to delete them myself."

"Okay," Avery said, "Strip and I'll give you the phone then."

Tye sat up and took off his shirt and tossed it aside. He next took off his jeans, now wearing only a pair of royal blue boxers.

"Happy?" Tye asked as he motioned at his body.

"Very," Avery said as he passed Tye his phone, "Your body still looks good."

"I was more defined back then," Tye said as he grabbed the phone, "I need to hit up a gym bad."

"You look good with a lil bit of extra weight on you," Avery said, "I'm surprised you wear boxers."

Tye deleted the photos and tossed the phone aside, "I don't actually. These belong to a friend."

"What?" Avery questioned as he furrowed his brows, "A friend?"

"Yeah," Tye said, "I have this friend who's into some freaky shit. He likes wearing dirty boxers. So I've been wearing these for him."

"Are you fucking this friend?" Avery asked.

"That is none of your business," Tye said.

Avery rubbed at Tye's abs, "Man, if he's fucking you, I'm jealous."

"Avery, you're blowing my mind tonight," Tye said, "This is a very crazy start to the new year."

Avery sat up and took off his shirt, revealing his scrawny body and hairy chest. He took off his pants, only wearing a pair of white briefs. Avery was sporting a hard on that had to stretch at least nine inches. Tye imagined the man having a long dick and tonight that was confirmed.

"Are you trying to show off?" Tye asked as he looked down at Avery's dick.

"I'm just getting comfortable," Avery said.

Tye scratched his fingers at Avery's hairy chest, "You really need to shave, my dude."

"It's pointless," Avery said, "It grows right back. It's like that everywhere, see."

Avery lifted the strap of his briefs, revealing his bushy pubes and his long brown dick. His dick head was almost pointed a bit. Avery decided to remove his briefs completely and his dick flopped down against his stomach, stretching all the way pass his navel.

"Damn," Tye voiced, "That is a big fucking dick."

Avery laughed, "You think so?"

"I know so," Tye said, "Your wife is lucky as hell."

"She doesn't even give head," Avery said.

"She's so damn ungrateful," Tye said.

Avery moved some pillows aside, "Do you mind if I bust a nut right quick?"

"Um...it's your house," Tye said.

Avery removed aside enough pillows to reveal the bottom surface of the bed. He opened a hatch revealing a small space that had some weed, condoms, lube, and cigarettes inside. Avery removed a condom and covered the hatch with some pillows. He slipped the condom halfway down his long dick and started to slowly jerk off.

"Hiding things from your wife?" Tye asked.

"Yup," Avery said.

"Why are you jerking off with a condom?" Tye asked.

"Because nut is incredibly hard to get out of these pillows," Avery said, "You want to join in?"

"I'm cool," Tye said.

"Are you just going to watch me then?" Avery asked.

Tye didn't want to watch him. He wanted to get fucked by him. But Tye needed to be extremely careful about sleeping with people who were close to his father. If Shelia ever found out about this, even though it was all Avery's doing, he was sure his father would catch some of the heat. But never have Tye encountered a dick like Avery's.

"How bad do you want me?" Tye asked.

"Bad," Avery said.

"If you ever say anything, this can ruin everything," Tye said.

"Including my marriage and what's left of my career," Avery said, "It'll be stupid of me to open my mouth about this."

15

"Fine," Tye said.

"Stand up," Avery said, "And drop those boxers slow for me."

Tye stood up and did his best to stay balanced on the bed of pillows. As requested, he slowly started to remove his boxers. Avery jerked off slow, watching Tye close. Tye dropped the boxers into the center of the bed of pillows.

Avery looked to them, "You want me to fuck you on your boxers for your friend, huh?"

"He would like that," Tye said.

"Are you going to tell me who this mystery man is yet?" Avery asked.

"I'm very good at keeping secrets," Tye said, "So, no."

"Turn around for me," Avery commanded.

Tye turned around revealing his booty to Avery. "Like this."

Avery jerked his dick harder, "I've wanted to see your ass up close for so fucking long. You have no idea how beautiful everything about you is. I fucking hate the place I'm at in my life, married to a woman that I love but don't want. If we could stay in this room forever it would be so fucking perfect."

Tye looked back at Avery, "Wow."

"I'm sorry," Avery said, "But I want you so fucking bad. Get down here."

The moment Tye lay back on the bed, Avery tackled him. The man started kissing all over Tye and rubbing at his hole. Tye didn't waste any time reaching down to grab a handful of Avery's long dick. He could feel all those passionate words Avery spoke being unleashed through his actions. The man was not giving Tye a chance to breathe or get comfortable. Every moment, every second, Avery's hands and lips were somewhere on Tye's body.

"I can't wait to stick my dick into you," Avery said.

"Just fucking do it already then," Tye said as he managed to get flat on his back and spread his legs.

Avery took his long dick and started to push into Tye inch by inch, "Oh shit, oh shit, oh shit."

Tye through his legs in the air, "Keep pushing that dick in."

"I wanted your ass for so damn long," Avery said.

"You got it now," Tye said, "Fuck it hard."

"You like it hard?" Avery asked.

"Make me beg you to stop," Tye challenged.

Avery started to stroke his long dick in and out of Tye. Tye wished they had started this sooner instead of all the chit chatting, because Avery stroke game was delivering strong right now. Avery's stroke game was the definition of getting some good dick. Tye loved how hard Avery was going in on his hole and the way the man was pressing down on his chest with his forearm.

Tye stared Avery into his eyes, "You love this ass, huh?"

"It's better than all the pussy in the world," Avery declared.

"I want you to fuck me until my ass gets wet," Tye said, "You think you can do that?"

Avery started to pump harder and deeper into Tye, "You trying to fuck up my pillows?"

Tye laughed, "Fuck your pillows."

Avery came down and kissed Tye, "Even your lips are tasty as fuck. Smile for me."

Tye smiled up at Avery and the man brought his tongue down and licked at his teeth.

Tye sat up a bit and hugged his body close to Avery's scrawny torso. Them being so close together started to make them both start to sweat. Avery's started to sweat from his forehead, it dripping down Tye's back. The forty-five year old was managing to keep up though, his stroke game not easing up at all. Each time Avery stroked deep, Tye let out a loud moan. He wanted the world to watch them fuck.

"You should've come up and fuck me," Tye said.

"Huh?"

"If you wanted me so bad the first day you saw me, you should've come up to my room and fuck me," Tye said.

Avery laughed, "You wanted me to end up on the news?"

"Admit it," Tye said, "This ass is worth a few years."

Avery laughed and flipped Tye over to his stomach, "Fuck that jail shit, unless you were my bottom bitch."

Avery slipped his dick back into Tye and pumped him from behind. Tye arched his booty and kept throwing his ass back. He loved it when Avery got all of his dick into him, down to his balls. Feeling the man's hairy balls slapping up against him from behind made Tye want to bust.

"Is this a good way to start off the year or what?" Avery asked as he forced all his weight down on Tye.

"It'll be better if you nut on my face," Tye said.

Avery pulled out of Tye and stood up on the bed of pillows, "You really want to fuck up my pillows, huh?"

Tye got on his knees, "They'll be fine if you got good aim."

17

Tye opened his mouth wide. Avery tore off his condom and started to jerk off. He managed to stick half of his dick in Tye's mouth and still had a good couple of inches left to use his hand to jerk off. From side to side, Tye slid his tongue against the man's dick shaft waiting to taste his nut in his throat.

"I'm about to drown your ass," Avery said, "Here it comes."

A warm shot of nut hit the back of Tye's throat. More of Avery's nut flowed out as the man moaned and his scrawny body flexed. Tye kept gulping down as fast as he could. He reached out and grabbed Avery's balls, squeezing them, wanting as much nut as possible in his throat. No more nut to give, Avery pulled his dick out of Tye's mouth. Before Tye could swallow the nut he had left in his mouth, Avery leaned over and kissed him. Avery started to eat some of his own nut from Tye's mouth. No more nut to share, Avery stood upright, panting in ecstasy.

Tye grabbed his boxers and placed them between his booty cheeks, "Damn that was good."

Avery laughed, "Happy fucking New Year's."

Tye wasn't done, Avery's hanging balls were looking snack worthy. He pulled the man close and munched on his balls. He did not care what anybody in Riverbed would say if they saw him down on his knees, with balls deep in his mouth, naked. Tye refused to deny himself such a great pleasure tonight to please them.

18

3 - Soldier

Tye never got into the idea of sleeping with clothes on. For him, naked was always the best way to go. But this morning he wished he had slept with something on. The combination of his fan, the winter air outside, and his lack of clothing was making sleeping in late this morning nearly impossible. Though he didn't want to, Tye got up from his bed to go adjust the thermostat.

He poked his head out of his room door and could hear his father downstairs having an early morning group session with some of his clients. The man's New Year's party helped clear his reputation a bit, but he still had a long way to go before getting back on the good side of the local church community. Tye himself had a good new year's, still feeling some of the longest dick he took deep in him a week after it had happened. The hallway clear, Tye rushed from his bedroom into the hallway with his blanket wrapped around him.

He arrived to the thermostat and as he reached to adjust the temperature his blanket dropped halfway off his body, exposing a bit of his butt to the chilly hallway. From downstairs a guy with dreaded hair arrived to the hallway and was greeted by the sight of Tye's mocha booty.

Tye quickly glanced over his shoulder to learn that he wasn't alone in the hallway, "Shit."

The guy quickly looked away, "My bad, I was just looking for the upstairs bathroom."

"We have one downstairs," Tye said as he pulled up his blanket.

"I know," The guy quickly answered, "But it's not working and Mr. Herbert said I can use the one up here."

Tye recognized the guy from the New Year's party. He was one of the quiet ones who had been standing at the back of the group of his father's clients. Tye was well aware that his father's clients were off limits, he himself not wanting to mess with crazy again, but couldn't deny the cuteness of the guy who awkwardly stood before him.

"What's your name?" Tye asked.

"Dominique," He introduced, "But call me Dom."

"Alright, Dom," Tye said, "The bathroom is the second door down the hall."

"Alright, thanks," Dom said as he walked off toward the bathroom.

Tye looked over his shoulder to catch Dom staring back at him before slipping into the bathroom. If Dom wasn't off limits, Tye would've definitely dropped his blanket to give him a better look at his naked body. But Tye behaved himself and headed back to bed. He managed to get back to sleep and when he rolled over again it was around noon. Tye slipped on some dark green sweatpants and made his way downstairs scratching at his toned bicep.

Tye entered the kitchen to find his father reading at the kitchen table, "Which book is that?"

"Harry Potter," Herbert said as he licked his finger before turning a page.

Tye grabbed an apple from the fruit bowl and joined his father at the table, "Why?"

Herbert laughed, "Because sometimes I like to escape. Unlike your mother, I can escape to the pages of a good book, not an entire country."

Tye bit into his apple, "She's doing good, helping the needy."

"And sleeping with whom?" Herbert asked, "I know you know, son."

Tye believe the man in the photo his mother texted to him was Rodrigo, "I have no idea," He lied.

"Liar," Herbert said as he closed his book, "What are you doing today?"

"I'm going to see an old professor of mine who's in town," Tye said, "You?"

"I'm going down to the church to audition for the black history month play," Herbert said, "I want to play which ever civil rights leader was bald and has the fewest amount of lines. Even though my group session this morning was a success, I would like to have more clients on my roster. And getting the church back on my side will do just that."

"Do you remember when I played Martin Luther King in that play?" Tye asked.

"How old were you...ten?" Herbert asked.

"Yup, way before being branded the town ho," Tye said, "So much has changed."

"For the better," Herbert said, "I'm proud of who you are son."

"I'm proud of you too, dad," Tye said as he finished his apple, "So, any interesting new clients?"

Tye specifically wanted to know more about Dom even though he shouldn't have wanted too.

"I can't give much details, but just know like always, many of their problems would be gone if they had money or a true friend to talk too," Herbert said, "I can be that friend but I cannot put money in their pockets. I can only encourage them to dig their boots out of the hood of Riverbed and strive for better. Half will work hard, the other half will need a lot more pushing unless they'll end up on welfare, dead, or in jail. I'll push them hard."

"I know you will," Tye said as he stood up from the table, "I'm going to go put on some clothes, pops."

"Is this meeting with your professor related to you getting back into school?" Herbert asked.

"I'm in the school of life for now," Tye voiced as he rushed off upstairs.

Tye stripped out of his sweat pants and put on the same boxers he had been wearing for the last two weeks, the same boxers Avery had fucked him on. He put on dark jeans, a black t-shirt, and one of his many snapbacks, this one bright red, and combat boots. By the time Tye left the house his father had already headed over to the church to audition for the black history play. Tye still had some guilt dwelling within him.

His father wouldn't have to be auditioning for a play he had no interest in being in if he hadn't slept with the man's client. For a moment Tye wondered if he himself should be auditioning for the play, but was sure he wouldn't get casted because of who he was. Plus, he had much better things to be doing like catching up with his favorite professor.

Tye hopped in his car and drove over to the CSU campus where he once lived and was the part-time residence of Perry, the on and off public speaking professor. After making his way across campus by foot, Tye arrived to the red brick, staff housing home where Perry lived. Tye knocked on the door and a tall, dark, buff, and handsome Perry answered wearing only black gym shorts. The army veteran yanked Tye into his home and slammed the door closed.

"Have you missed me?" Tye asked as he smiled at Perry.

Perry hoisted Tye up, threw him over his shoulder, and smacked him on the ass, "Too damn much."

Perry charged up the stairs of his home carrying Tye on his arms as if he was weightless. The man arrived to his bedroom, set Tye down on his feet, and started to unbuckle his jeans. Tye took off his shirt and kicked off his shoes as Perry pulled his jeans down for him. Once Tye was stripped down just to the pair of dirty boxes, Perry dropped to his knees. The man shoved his nose into Tye's crotch and inhaled deeply.

Tye laughed as he rubbed at Perry's block head of buzzcut hair, "Perry, relax."

Perry looked up at Tye cheesing, "How long did you wear these?"

"About two weeks," Tye revealed, "I even got fucked on them."

Perry grabbed a handful of Tye's ass and pulled his dick out of the boxers, "Are you for real?"

"I'm for real," Tye said.

Perry shoved Tye's dick in his mouth and sucked on it until it got hard. He kept grabbing at Tye's ass and deep throating his dick. Accustomed to Perry's aggressive ways, Tye just stood letting the man take control. Perry pulled his lips from around Tye's dick and stuck his tongue into his dick hole. A mixture of spit and precum formed a line from Perry's tongue to Tye's dick as the man slowly pulled back.

Perry stood from his knees and kissed Tye, "How have you been doing?"

"Still trying to help my dad fix his reputation. How about you soldier?" Tye asked.

"I spent the last month in Florida giving group after group of punk ass high schoolers inspirational speeches," Perry said, "Half of them texted the entire time I told them about my tour in Iraq and how someday they could be a hero like me and all of that bullshit. It was a good trip though. I got about ten of them to enlist. Still, getting back here to Riverbed was the only thing truly on my mind."

"Did you bring me a gift?" Tye jokingly asked.

Perry dropped his boxers to the floor, revealing his veiny black dick and the silver cockring he wore around it. Tye grabbed at the man's fat dick and ran his hand up and down the shaft. This was so much better than a t-shirt. Perry tore a hole in Tye's dirty boxers and shoved him backward onto his bed. He managed to fit a condom on his bulging dick, climbed into bed, yank Tye's legs opened, and stroked into him.

"Motherfucker," Perry screamed as if he was angry at the world, "Fuck!"

Tye let out a loud moan as the man started to aggressively fuck him. Since day one sex with Perry was rough and strange. The man was actually Tye's first ever fuck as a college student. Tye had went to a local gay bar, flirted with Perry while doing some underage drinking, watched the man do coke in the bathroom, and then got fucked by him in a stall. It wasn't until the next day Tye found himself sore and sitting in the soldier's public speaking class. Everybody loved a bad boy and Tye just couldn't get enough of the coke sniffing, steroid taking, dirty underwear loving, soldier.

Perry lifted Tye up from the bed and stroked into his hole as he stood holding him in his arms. A strong Perry, lifted Tye from his dick, all the way over his shoulders, and sat his hole on his mouth. He continued to hold Tye up as he ate out his hole. Tye was afraid he would be dropped but was turned on so much at the same time. Perry dropped Tye back to his bed and flipped him over onto his stomach. He tore the hole in Tye's boxers even wider, before mounting him from behind and shoving his dick back into him.

"You're a good D student, huh?" Perry asked as he stroked deep into Tye.

"Yes teacher," Tye moaned out, "I love getting a D from you."

"I'm going to make you feel this big...black....D....all the way in your stomach," Perry said.

"Deeper teacher," Tye begged, "What can I do for extra credit?"

Perry let out a crazy laugh as he tore of Tye's dirty boxers. The man pulled his dick from Tye's hole and started to finger fuck him with the boxers wrapped around his hand. Perry took the boxers and shoved them into his own mouth. The man stood upright near the bed, with his hands behind his back, and the boxers in his mouth.

Tye slid from the bed to his knees before Perry's dick. He removed the tightly fitted condom and stuck the soldier's dick into his mouth. As Tye sucked Perry's dick the soldier let out muffled screams and remained standing at attention. Tye loved how he could feel almost every vein of the man's dick against his lips as he slid them up and down his shaft.

Perry spat the boxers from his mouth, "Motherfucker here it comes!"

A giant mess of nut shot from Perry's dick onto Tye's face. Tye had to close his eyes because of all the nut that kept pouring out from the man's dick. Perry finally broke his stance as he pressed his strong hands against the top of Tye's head as he continued to nut all over his face. Tye just took all the nut the man had all over his face until he was forced to his feet.

Perry started kissing all over Tye, sucking up his own nut. He forced Tye to open up his mouth and spat all of his nut out on his tongue. Tye gladly swallowed it all, Perry always managing to bring out the freak in him. Perry dropped to his knees once again and gently teased Tye's balls with his finger tips and sucked at his dick. The way Perry sucked dick was so calming, which was surprising coming from such an aggressive man.

"I'm going to nut," Tye warned.

Perry opened his mouth like a baby bird waiting to be fed and jerked Tye off. Tye started to pant heavily as nut poured from his dick and down Perry's throat. Perry kept his mouth full of nut as he sucked on Tye's dick a bit longer before finally swallowing it all down. Perry got up, shared a kiss with Tye, and shoved him back down on his bed.

Perry paced around the room rolling his neck, "And that's why I fuck with you."

"That was everything," Tye said as he softly laughed.

Perry sat on his room floor and pulled his knees to his chest, "I just want to stare at you."

Tye got up onto his knees, "Why?"

"Because you're beautiful," Perry said, "The perfect fuck. I want you to grab those boxers, stay on your knees, and finger yourself for me until I tell you to stop, okay? I just want to watch you make love to yourself."

Tye grabbed the boxers and started to make love to himself for the man. Perry watched for a bit but eventually grabbed a tin box from his end table drawer and started sniffing coke. Tye kept performing for the man until Perry got up, snatched the boxers from him, and put them on himself. The man stood wearing the torn boxers that could barely contain his big thick dick.

He ran his hand down Tye's face, "You drive safe, okay?"

"You don't want me to spend the night?" Tye asked.

Perry touched at the boxers, "I just want to have fun with these tonight."

"Do you want me to start a new pair?"

"Yeah," Perry said, "But this time wear a thong. Keep it deep between those ass cheeks for me, okay?"

"I will," Tye said as he got up from the bed.

As he started to get dressed, Perry crawled into the bed and started to slowly jerk his dick while rubbing at his muscled body. Tye once witnessed the man edge his dick for nearly an entire night. He decided to leave Perry to enjoy himself and returned home to find his father in the living room strolling through Netflix.

Tye shut the house door, "How was the audition?"

"I'm playing Martin Luther King," Herbert said, "The bald version."

"You're following in my footsteps on stage, huh?" Tye teased.

Herbert let out a sigh as he said, "Sadly."

Tye laughed as he headed upstairs, ready to get some sleep after all that Perry had just taken his body through. He locked his room door as he entered and raised his window blinds. Next door,

Avery sat before the window of his man cave, wearing headphones and holding his long dick in his hands.

Slowly, Tye started to get naked as the man watched him and jerked off. Tye pressed his ass up against his room window and revealed his hole to Avery. He looked over his shoulder to spot Avery busting a nut all over himself. Once the man was finished, Tye lowered his blinds and crawled into bed naked.

4 - Distance

Tye sat on Perry's couch naked with his legs sprawled open while the man was down on his knees eating his ass. Perry, who only wore the pair of tattered boxers, had shoved four Skittles deep into Tye's hole and wasn't going to stop until he got them all out. He had already managed to fish out two of them using his tongue and was working up a sweat as he tried to retrieve the remainder. Tye lay back relaxing as he let the man worked and stared at all of the photos Perry had on the wall from his pre-Iraq days. Perry rarely talked about his past, but based on some of his photos he was your typical high school jock who went to prom with a girl who he looked to have little interest it.

"I got that son of a bitch," Perry said.

Perry opened his mouth revealing a yellow Skittle, chewed it, swallowed it down and went back to work searching for the last one. Based on the way Perry kept thrusting his muscled leg back and kicking his coffee table, he was getting frustrated. His physical frustration got verbal and he started to cuss under his breath. Perry dug two fingers into Tye's hole and reached around inside of him.

"Dude, can you try not to destroy my walls," Tye said as he tried to pull Perry's fingers out of him.

"My dick is fat enough to fill any hole," Perry said.

"But you're not going to be the only guy I fuck for the rest of my life," Tye said.

"I should be," Perry said as he fought to get his fingers deeper into Tye.

"But you won't be," Tye said, "We're not boyfriends."

"What the fuck are we again?" Perry asked before he went down and sucked on Tye's hole.

"Friends," Tye said as his eyes rolled into the back of his head, "Really...fucking...good friends."

"I got it," Perry said.

He opened his mouth revealing a red Skittle that had lost most of his color.

"Finally," Tye said.

"It's never taken that long," Perry said, "But it's all a part of your training."

"My training?" Tye questioned as he closed his legs.

"In the future I want you to be able to push out whatever I put up there," Perry said.

"Basically, you want to train me to squirt," Tye said.

Perry nodded as he remained on his knees, "Are you down with that?"

"I guess," Tye said, "But it'll be a long process. You're never here."

"Because I have to do my duty and recruit the future soldiers of America," Perry said.

"Who do you fuck when you're on the road?" Tye asked.

Perry laughed, "What makes you think I fuck other people?"

"You're the freakiest person I know," Tye said, "I can't imagine you saving yourself for me."

"I fuck strangers, a couple of my fellow soldiers, and even some new recruits," Perry revealed, "I find these strangers on the same apps I'm sure you use, I know the fellow soldiers from serving with them, and as for the new recruits, I just invite them over, get them drunk, and sweet talk them into getting naked for me at their own will."

"Nobody's at their own will around you," Tye said, "You got me to put Skittles in my ass."

Perry burst out laughing, "Are you saying I'm a master manipulator?"

"Your kink rubs off on those in your presence" Tye said.

Perry thought about it for a moment, "I guess...that's sort of true."

"Tell me some stories from the road," Tye said, "Tell me about a time you fucked a stranger?"

Perry rubbed at his square jaw as he thought back, "I had just arrived in Charlotte. And I was so hard that my dick was leaking nut the entire drive down. The first thing I did was booted up one of those apps and got hit up by this really scrawny guy who was around twenty-four I think. And his name was Benson. He wasn't looking for sex, but was instead trying to recruit gay men like himself to come and volunteer down at a homeless shelter. In my head, my dick was already deep in him and I could not let him slip away."

"You're animal," Tye said as he softly laughed.

"I went down to this homeless shelter and of course I was the only guy he managed to recruit," Perry said, "After ten minutes I was ready to go. Dirty people were coughing, scratching, and just staring at me and that shit was making me uncomfortable. But I could not leave without sticking my dick into this guy who had me serving soup and shit. Benson and I went out back to dump some trash. And I made my move. I built him up, telling him how proud of him I was, how much good he was doing, and that I was going to use my military connections to put him in touch with some charitable organizations I previously worked with."

"And was that all a lie?" Tye asked.

"Of course," Perry said, "And he ate it all up. I told him to let me suck his dick and I would put him on the phone with one of those charities ASAP. He agreed. I texted a friend of mine and gave him a heads up about the call, pulled out Benson's dick while my friend chatted him up, and by the end of their conversation he was convinced that an organization would be donating some of their resources to which ever event he had planned next. Benson's spirit was so high and my head game so good that he didn't even bother to stop me from stripping him naked and fucking him behind the dumpster. I spat so much nut all over him."

"I'm turned off and on at the same time," Tye said, "Who's your sick friend that went along with this plan?"

"One of the soldiers I jerk off with when I'm on the road," Perry said, "We always look out for each other."

"Have you ever fucked this soldier?" Tye asked.

"No, but we suck each other's dicks all the time when we cross paths," Perry said.

"I'm afraid to even ask what you've done with some of the recruits," Tye said.

"They're the easiest but the most risky," Perry said, "You have to make sure they initiate everything. I've seen a couple of close friends lose it all because some recruit cried rape even when they tried to pass it off as just hazing. The last one I was with basically begged me for nearly an hour to suck his dick. I told him some crazy stories just like the one I just told you tonight."

"I still don't see how stories like these can turn a straight boy out," Tye said.

"First, I tell them these fucked up stories are only stuff that can be shared between brothers, so they immediately feel included and a part of something bigger," Perry said, "And then I basically sell them on the idea that it's not gay if you're the one getting your dick sucked. Then you give them some liquid courage and cross your fingers. Some avoid me like the plague after we're done chatting while others find themselves shoving their dicks into my mouth."

"As I said, you bring out everybody's kink," Tye said, "When are you leaving again?"

"Tomorrow morning," Perry said.

"For how long?" Tye asked.

"I don't know," Perry said, "But you know I'll be ready for you when I get back."

Tye stood up from the couch, his hard dick poking out in Perry's face.

Perry grabbed at Tye's hard dick, "What's this?"

"Your stories got me all hard," Tye said.

"Do you want me to take care of this before you leave?" Perry asked.

"Don't act as if you were going to let me leave this way in the first place," Tye said.

Perry smirked and stuck Tye's dick into his mouth. The man jerked his own dick as it hung from the torn boxers as he kept on giving Tye some nice, slow, soothing head. Tye rubbed his hands at Perry's head of buzzcut hair. He could only imagine the tons of crazy stories the soldier had buried deep in his mind. Tye was sure the conversations between them would never end. Tye pushed Perry's head down on his dick as he started to nut in his mouth. Perry didn't remove his lips from Tye's dick until he got every last bit of nut out of him.

Tye pulled his dick from Perry's mouth and kissed him on the forehead, "Be nice on your road trip."

Perry laughed, "I'll try. And don't forget about the thong, okay?"

"I won't," Tye said, "Bye, Perry."

Tye got dressed and left the soldier's home.

5 - Martin

The church's black history play had become another excuse for the black elite of Riverbed to gather, boast, and network. It was basically the same play that was put on every year, only the actors changing. And tonight Tye's father was the star. The man put in a lot of work when it came to his role, even though he didn't want too. But Herbert knew a good performance tonight could get him back on the church's good side.

The only reason Tye decided to show up to the play was because unlike the previous years, the venue was off church property. Because the event attracted so many attendees, it was moved to a ballroom. Tye hated that his father would have to jump through so many hoops before the play's biggest audience to date. While the play was underway, like most in attendance, Tye paid little attention to it. He had watched his father rehearse around the house long enough to know the man's lines word by word.

Most of those from the church who built this play up as if it was the second coming weren't even paying attention themselves. Instead they were walking around eating, laughing, and throwing Tye the side eye. Tye heard a couple of whispers about his outfit, deciding to only wear a denim jacket, khakis, a white t-shirt, and high top sneakers instead of dressing up.

But Tye knew for sure that one person who was interested in his outfit was Preacher Ramsey and his wife Glenda's pride and joy, Isaiah. Tye couldn't lie, he was packing on a few pounds which made his pants fit a bit tight in certain areas. And based on the way Isaiah kept staring at him from across the room, Tye's butt was looking especially nice in his khakis. According to Avery, Isaiah was a big fan of Tye and even had those leaked photos of him saved on his phone. Tye had no desire of giving Isaiah any of his time or attention. After a night of feeling like an outcast, Tye finally bumped into a friendly face.

Avery, who wore a loose fitting, dark suit, approached Tye and shook his hand, "Your dad is killing it."

"Yet nobody is watching," Tye said.

"I sat down for the first five minutes," Avery said with a smirk.

"You lasted longer than me," Tye said, "He gets shot in the end, we get a black president, racism is over."

Avery laughed, "You're funny. And look so fucking damn sexy tonight."

Tye looked around to make sure nobody overheard Avery, "Thanks."

Avery leaned in closed and whispered, "I want to fuck you with nothing but your sneakers on."

"I'm starting to think your wife is not here tonight, huh?" Tye asked as he looked around the packed ballroom for her.

"Nope, working," Avery said, "The perfect time for us to head back to the man cave."

"I'm my dad's ride home," Tye said, "I can't leave him."

"Then there has to be somewhere we can fuck in here," Avery said.

"Or we can meet up at the man cave at another time," Tye said.

"But I want you right now, sneakers on, deep on my dick," Avery said, "It's been torture just watching you undress every night. I want another taste of the real thing and I cannot leave her tonight without sticking my dick deep into you. Don't act as if you don't want all of this long dick tonight."

Tye could not deny that. He looked around the ballroom and his eyes landed on the one place that would be abandoned during a church funded event, the bar. The preacher's wife did not allow any drinking period at these events. Tye discreetly nodded over to the set of doors that led to the bar area and made the first move. The bathrooms were through the same door so it made slipping into the area easy. He continued into the darkened bar area and ducked down behind the bar. It wasn't long before Avery joined him.

Tye overheard his father starting his final monologue of the play, "We have about ten minutes before the play ends."

Avery loosened his tie and started to unfasten his belt, "Then let's hurry the fuck up."

As fast he could Tye stripped out of his clothes down to just his high-top sneakers. That gave Avery more than enough time to slip on a condom. Tye got in a face down ass up position as they remained hidden behind the bar and Avery stroked his long dick into him. The man wrapped his scrawny arms around Tye and started to fuck him. Avery smacked on a piece of minted scented gum in Tye's ear.

"I wish we had more time," Avery whispered in Tye's ear.

"Fuck, me too," Tye said as he started to throw his ass back.

Avery hugged his arms tighter around Tye as he started to nut, "Oh yeah, that shit feels so damn good."

The audience out in the ballroom started to clap. Avery dick's still in him, Tye grabbed his clothes and started to get dressed. He got his shirt and jacket back on first and once Avery pulled out, put on his khakis. Avery gave him a quick kiss and left the bar. Tye waited for a couple of minutes before heading out after Avery and joined the crowd as they cleared out the ballroom. As Tye arrived outside, his father was shaking hands with Preacher Ramsey and his wife. He purposely took his slow time to walk over to his father until the preacher and his wife had walked away.

Tye approached his dad, "You were a star up there."

Herbert rolled his eyes, "Yeah, right. I would've rather been getting drunk with you and Avery."

"Huh? What do you mean?"

Herbert wagged his finger at Tye and winked, "I saw you two sneak off into the bar. But I don't blame you two, a night like this needed alcohol. But it's all over with and I'm one step closer to getting back on the church's good side. They're already asking me to sponsor a golden egg for the Easter Ball. Of course I'm going to do it."

Tye was relieved his father only thought him and Avery were drinking, "You ready to get out of here?"

"Yeah," Herbert said, "I have an early morning session scheduled."

Tye and Herbert left the ballroom property, headed home, and got some sleep. The next morning Tye was awoken once again by a freezing house. He refused to get rid of his fan, the white noise helping him sleep. His father acted like a middle aged woman going through menopause so always kept the AC on full blast when he slept. Tye got out of bed to go adjust the thermostat and went into the hallway to find his father rushing out of his room.

Tye yawned, "Where are you going?"

"Preacher Ramsey has invited the cast of the play down to the church for breakfast," Herbert said, "I'm going to rush on down and show my face. Push my morning session back an hour. I won't be long. All the information is in my planner."

Tye nodded, "Okay."

Herbert rushed downstairs and out of the home. Tye adjusted the thermostat and went to search for his father's planner. He kept the blanket wrapped tight around himself as he searched all the usual places but could not find the book anywhere. Tye started to call his father but there was a knock on the door. He wrapped the blanket tighter as he went to answer the door to find a dreaded hair Dom standing on the porch. Dom wore some baggy jeans, timberland boots, and a violet hoody.

"Yo," Dom said as his eyes struggled to stay locked on Tye.

"My dad isn't here," Tye said.

"But we were supposed to be meeting at nine," Dom said as he rubbed at the back of his neck.

"He won't be back for another hour," Tye said.

"Well...can I just wait," Dom said, "I caught the bus up here."

Tye wanted to get back to bed not be a host, "Yeah, come on in."

He stepped aside and let Dom in the house.

Dom stared Tye down as he entered the house. He cleared his throat, "Um, so did you just wake up?"

"Yeah," Tye said, "Do you want anything to drink or something?"

"I'll take whatever," Dom said, "I'm not picky."

Tye dragged his blanket across the floor as he headed into the kitchen. "We have orange juice."

"That'll work," Dom said as he followed after Tye.

Tye did his best to keep the blanket over his naked body as he poured Dom some orange juice.

"Is it true what they say about you?" Dom nervously asked as he sat at the kitchen table.

Tye softly laughed as he set the glass of orange juice on the table, "What do they say?"

"That you fuck with dudes," Dom said in a low voice as if he thought somebody would overhear him.

"Yeah, that's true and everything they add on is an exaggeration or lie," Tye said, "Why do you care?"

"I-I-I-I was just asking," Dom uttered out.

Tye had a strong feeling that Dom wasn't just asking, "Do you have a girlfriend?"

"Nah," Dom said, "I have so much going on in my life right now."

Tye didn't believe that for a second.

"What's your story Dom?" Tye asked, "If you don't mind me asking, why is my father counseling you?"

"I'm looking for guidance, a way out of a messy situation, and trying to break away from my fucked up dad, but without abandoning my little sisters," Dom said, "So, don't stand there thinking I'm crazy or some shit. I've heard about how your dad helped a lot of people and came to him seeking help...that's all. Why is your father counseling you?"

"He's not counseling me," Tye said as he sat the glass of orange juice on the table, "I work for him. I'm fine."

"Even after all that shit about your photos being on Facebook?"

"It made my life difficult but I'm surviving," Tye said, "Have you seen the photos?"

"Oh hell no," Dom quickly answered as he fidgeted around in his seat.

Tye softly laughed at how uncomfortable Dom looked, "I mean...I won't be mad if you did."

"I didn't," Dom snapped as he stood up and got in Tye's face, "I'm not into that gay shit."

Tye leaned back from Dom, "Alright, relax. You brought up this topic not me."

"I just wanted to know more about you, your truth," Dom explained.

"My truth is simple," Tye said, "I'm just trying to make sure I don't ruin my dad's career. Which means I should not be sleeping with his clients, telling them my business, or getting into any fights with them. So please do me a favor and have a seat. My father will be back soon."

Dom nodded as he sat back down, "I'm sorry."

Tye all of a sudden started to feel bad for him, "I didn't mean to come off as mean or anything."

36

"No, I shouldn't be in your business," Dom said.

Tye felt as if Dom had more than just daddy issues. If he could help a client of his father come out, he would try without really getting too involved. Tye could tell by the way Dom barely could stare at him or how uneasy he made him that there was something more on his tongue that he wanted to say to him, something he wanted to admit to somebody who may understand.

"You were being social," Tye said, "And I'm not used to that from most guys who talk to me."

"Why not?" Dom asked.

"To be blunt," Tye said, "Most guys who approach me just want to get me naked."

Dom rubbed his hands at his thighs, "That doesn't make them bad."

Tye softly laughed, "Nope, not at all. I just think it's unfair that they've all seen me naked, exposed, and it's never the other way around. Because of a stupid decision I've lost all my sexual mystery. While everybody else like you get to keep there's hidden beneath their clothes and in their bedroom."

"I'm sorry to hear that," Dom said.

Tye smirked at him, "Stop apologizing and drink your orange juice."

Tye made his way from the kitchen and looked over his shoulder to find Dom sipping his orange juice and looking over to him. Though having no mystery came with some cons, there were plenty of pros. Men like Avery were easier to attract and they loved opening up to Tye. He felt this morning Dom was attempting to do the same.

6 - Purchase

Tye stood naked in his bathroom using his clippers to touch up his haircut. He had a pretty long drive planned for today. He needed to go find the perfect thong to wear for Perry. There were plenty of options online but Tye didn't see the problem with driving out to a sex shop to do some browsing. There was a knock on his bedroom door.

"Are you decent?" Herbert asked from the hallway.

Tye quickly slipped on his briefs from the bathroom floor, "Yeah, I'm in my bathroom."

Herbert entered the room and walked over to the bathroom wearing khaki slacks, a pressed red dress shirt, and smelling like aftershave. The man's mocha skin was oiled up. Tye could only stare his father up and down wondering where he was going this early so dressed up.

"I have a client coming over this morning," Herbert said.

"Aren't you a bit overdressed?" Tye said as he put away his clippers.

"This is my biggest client in a long time," Herbert said, "I need to go above and beyond."

"Who is it?" Tye asked, "The mayor? Because his crazy ass needs a ton of help."

Herbert laughed, "No, this person is more important than the mayor."

"Tell me dad," Tye said as he narrowed his eyes at the man, done with the guessing game.

"Isaiah," Herbert revealed.

Simply hearing the name made Tye feel exposed, "As in Preacher Ramsey's son?"

"Yeah," Herbert said, "He's coming over in about an hour. His parents approved all of this. This is my first big client that's related to the church. If this goes perfectly, I know I'm going to be back in with them. I'm going to give Isaiah everything I have to offer plus more."

"Is he coming to talk about his sexual confusion?" Tye asked, knowing his photos was on the man's phone.

"No," Herbert answered, confused to why Tye would ask that, "His spending problems."

"Oh, so you're telling me that the BMW and all his nice clothes aren't gifts from above?" Tye sarcastically asked.

"Don't make those types of jokes around him," Herbert stressed, "I need to build a successful relationship with Isaiah and if convincing him to cut up his credit cards and ban him from going to the mall does that, I will. I'm sure his obsessive shopping is connected to his parents somehow but we'll see when he gets here. Are you going to stick around to say hi to him?"

Tye stepped out of the bathroom pass his father, "I have to go somewhere."

"Where?" Herbert asked.

"I just need to go outside sometimes," Tye said as he slipped on some jeans.

"Are you okay?" Herbert asked, "I know you had a tough year last year."

"No, you had a tough year," Tye said, "And it was my fault. I'm fine dad. Just worry about your clients."

"Speaking of clients, thanks for letting Dominique in yesterday," Herbert said.

"I didn't mind," Tye said.

"What did you two talk about?" Herbert asked.

"His truth," Tye said, "And a bit about mine. Why?"

"Because I'm having the hardest time getting to him," Herbert said, "I think I'm coming off as too much as a father figure. And based on the shit he's dealing with now the last thing he wants is another father. I won't go into much detail about his private life, but the fact that he's let you in is promising. Maybe I need to be more of a friend to him."

Tye felt Dom only opened up to him because he wanted him to open up his legs, "Maybe."

Herbert wagged his finger in the air, "I'll figure him out. I always get to them in the end."

"And if he says anything else to me I'll let you know," Tye said.

"Just be careful," Herbert said, "I really don't like you getting too involved."

"I'm not going to sleep with him," Tye said.

"No, that is not my concern," Herbert said, "I just don't want you to get hurt."

"Is he dangerous?" Tye asked.

"We're all dangerous when the wrong buttons are pushed," Herbert said.

His father left his room and Tye continued to get dressed. He thought back to the moment when Dom got up in his face after he hinted at him possibly being gay. It was clear to Tye that was one of Dom's buttons that he should not push. He slipped on a navy blue shirt and a snapback to match and headed out. Since he now knew Isaiah would be coming over often he had to make sure to find something to do outside of the house. Though Avery was just as guilty for once having the pictures, at least he wasn't a hypocrite. Isaiah on the other hand was one of the many people who pushed for the out casting of Tye and his father from the community they were now slowly climbing their way back into.

Tye drove a bit outside of Riverbed, out of the suburbs, through the hood, to the far edge of town where you could find the trashiest bars and any type of drug you were looking for. He pulled up to a sex shop that sold everything from books to escorts. Tye headed inside and nodded at the tubby woman who sat at the register chewing gum and reading an erotica book. He headed over towards the attire section and browsed for some thongs. He had to make sure the thong he picked was comfortable but also absorbent enough to trap in everything Perry would want to taste when he would shove them into his mouth.

Across from Tye, browsing a shelf of body oils, he noticed a guy that looked just as out of place as him in this area. The dark skinned stranger wore a pair of fitted slacks, a white dress shirt that was unbuttoned at the top showing off his toned chest a bit, and a blazer. Everything about the dark stranger was sharp, from his nice shoes up to his fresh buzzcut hair.

They made eye contact and the well-dressed stranger smirked at Tye. Tye returned the gesture and refocused on shopping for some thongs. He grabbed three pairs to try on, a silk red thong, a black mesh thong, and a white g-string. Tye headed over to the dressing room area and noticed the dark stranger doing his best to discreetly follow after him. He arrived to the dressing room area only to learn all the changing booths were stuffed with boxes of inventory.

"This is some ratchet shit," Tye said as he looked around for somewhere more private to change.

He noticed out of the side of his eye the dark stranger had moved over to a stand of whips and chains that was near the dressing room area. Tye took the hint, he was being watched. He had never seen the stranger around Riverbed so figured he had to be traveling through the state or was from out of town. Tye found himself wanting to give the stranger a tour of one of the best features of Riverbed, himself.

He started to get undressed in the hallway of the dressing room area. Tye stripped naked before slipping on the red thong. The dark stranger smirked at Tye from a distance and gave him a thumbs up. Tye tried on the white g-string only for the dark stranger to shake his head in disapproval. Lastly, he tried on the black mesh thong that left little to the imagination.

The dark stranger made his way over toward Tye, "Perfect."

"I'm thinking the same thing," Tye said, "And it's the most comfortable."

"Because you're basically wearing nothing," The dark stranger said.

Tye tore the tag off the thong and passed it to the dark stranger, "You buying?"

"I don't know you like that," The dark stranger said with a smirk.

"I'm Tye," He introduced.

"Chaz," He said as he checked the price of the tag, "It's not that pricey."

"Don't act as if you couldn't afford it in the first place, rich boy," Tye teased.

"Why would you assume I have money?" Chaz asked.

"Because I live around people with money and you smell just like them," Tye said.

"People with money have a scent?" Chaz asked as he sniffed his blazer.

"Yup, bullshit," Tye quipped.

"If you live around people with money I assume you have a lot of it yourself," Chaz said.

"My father is pretty well off," Tye said, "I'm just on his payroll."

"Does he know you're out here stripping for strangers?" Chaz asked.

"I'm just trying some things on," Tye said, "You're the creep trying to get a free show."

"It's not free if I'm buying," Chaz said as he raised the price tag.

"What are you doing in here anyway?" Tye asked.

"I came to buy some oils," Chaz said, "I like to get all fancy when I touch myself."

"I swear you rich boys can never do anything small," Tye said, "So, you came for oils and..."

"That's it," Chaz said, "And then I looked up and saw you. You smirked at me and I just had to talk to you."

"What do you want to talk about then?" Tye asked as he crossed his arms.

"I want to talk about where you got the nerve to strip naked for a stranger," Chaz said.

"It's a long and tired story," Tye said, "Just know I'm not shy about showing some skin."

Chaz cautiously reached out and touched at Tye's waist, "I like you. You have a story."

"What's your story?" Tye asked.

"It's as long and tired as yours," Chaz said, "I'm straight."

Tye laughed, "Long and tired indeed. And I'm sure some girl you're dating believes that."

Chaz pushed up on Tye, "I don't care."

"That's cold," Tye said.

"Then tell me to leave you alone," Chaz said as he breathed heavily on Tye.

Tye agreed with Chaz, he needed to get away from him. He was already messing around with a married man, basically a future version of Chaz. The man before him today was nothing but a young Avery, prepping himself for a life of lies and marriage. Tye called Chaz cold, but could feel so much warmth coming from him. A warmth that the woman with Chaz was being denied.

"Are you going to ask me to leave you alone or not?" Chaz asked as he pushed Tye into a corner.

"You're making that very hard to do," Tye said.

Chaz shoved his hand into Tye's thong, "I'm not going to bring anything good to you."

"I know that," Tye said, "You'll leave me when you're done."

Chaz slipped two fingers into Tye's hole, "And you'll be hurt."

Tye rolled his eyes, "Trust me, I'll survive. Men like you never change."

Chaz pushed his fingers deeper into Tye, "Why do you say that?"

"Because I know a man who was like you once," Tye said, "Who thought marrying a woman would make him forget about guys like me. And just like you, he wants me more than any woman. I'll let you have your fun and I'll enjoy it along with you. I'll be absent for your days of misery. And another guy like me will catch your eye and bring you back into happiness. Your wife won't matter or your kids, just him."

Chaz laughed as he slowly stroked his fingers in and out of Tye, "Do you want to be friends?"

Tye leaned his head back and let out a moan.

"I'll take that as a 'yes'," Chaz said, "Do you promise to let me have my fun?"

"If you're asking me to not judge...then yes," Tye said.

Chaz pushed his fingers deeper into Tye, "Then apologize."

"For what?"

"For calling me cold," Chaz said, "Apologize."

Tye bit his bottom lip as he kept moaning.

"I said apologize," Chaz demanded.

"I'm sorry," Tye said, "I'm sorry that I hurt your feelings with the truth."

"I'll take that," Chaz said as he yanked his fingers out of Tye. He pulled his phone out of his pocket, "I want your number. And when I call you and need you to be there for me, I want you to do whatever you can to get to me. My schedule is tight, my family crowding, and my girl is smart. You'll have to be as smart as her."

Tye typed his number into Chaz's phone, "I can handle her, your family, and whatever else you have for me."

Chaz put his phone away, "I'm going to pay for your purchase. I'll call you Tye."

Chaz made his way out of the dressing room leaving Tye waiting for his call.

7 - Truth

Tye was a multitasker. And this skill was very needed for him at the moment. He found himself butt naked before his bedroom window, playing with himself for Avery and at the same time snapping photos to send to Chaz. It seemed as if Chaz wasn't lying about having a tight schedule. Since their meeting a week ago all he had time to do with Tye was text. His responses were vague and slow, but Tye knew exactly what Chaz wanted and that was to see him naked.

Tye knew sexting should be the last thing he should be doing, but Chaz was really good at luring him into the worst type of behavior. Tye looked across to Avery's man cave to find the man sitting on his knees near his bed of pillows pulling at his dick. Avery puckered his lips and blew a kiss over to Tye. Tye knew at some point and soon Chaz would vanish, but wondered how long Avery was going to put up with his behavior before retreating back to his wife.

Avery started to nut all over the floor of his man cave. Once the man was done, Tye closed his blinds, hit send on the text to Chaz and slipped on some clothes. He headed downstairs wearing just a pair of boxers and there was a knock on the door. He stopped to answer the door to find Isaiah on the porch. Isaiah wore an orange sweater vest over a light blue collar shirt, khakis, and light brown dress shoes. Last time Tye checked his father wasn't even home.

It took the usually charismatic Isaiah awhile to compose himself before a half-naked Tye, "Hi Tye."

"My dad isn't here," Tye said with a bit of an attitude.

"He's on his way here," Isaiah said as he forced his way into the home, "I'm having a session today. It's sort of a last minute thing."

"What's wrong with you?" Tye asked as he sat down on the living room couch.

Isaiah joined him, "I'm having some impulses I can't control."

"Pray on it," Tye sarcastically said as he turned on the television.

"I do," Isaiah said, "Every day. But I just can't stop buying stuff."

"Is that really your issue?" Tye asked.

"If you come over to my place you would understand," Isaiah said.

"I rather not," Tye said.

"It's funny," Isaiah said, "Because you once used to be really nice to me. We even used to eat lunch at school together."

Back then Tye had a major crush on Isaiah.

"I stopped being nice when you did," Tye said, "Just like your mother, you were trying to get me shunned from Riverbed. That's not cool at all. So don't expect me to sit here and smile in your face. You're a snake. A serpent in the garden."

"I wasn't in the position to support you," Isaiah said.

"What does that even mean?" Tye asked.

"In Riverbed it's all about status and positioning and you know that," Isaiah said, "I will soon be taking over my father's position in the church, becoming the youngest preacher in Riverbed, and must maintain the same influence and power he has over people. Supporting you and your lifestyle could jeopardize all of that. My position in the church is a lot more important than you getting to walk around town sleeping around with broken men."

Tye would punch Isaiah if his father didn't need him, "People think that way about me because others like you are going around saying the mess you just said. Let me set the record straight, this is not a brothel. Yes, I sleep with men, just like a lot of other people in this town. And I feel as if I was only attacked to make everybody else feel good about their shitty lives. You were all taking your hate for yourselves out on me. I'm happy though, while people like you for example are seeking counseling."

Isaiah laughed, "You're not happy. You have no faith in your life."

Tye tried to play nice, "Why are you always looking at me?"

"Excuse me," Isaiah said as he cleared his throat.

"I want to know why every time we're in a room together your eyes are on me," Tye said, "What about me makes me so damn interesting that you just can't look away? Are you judging me? Are you in disgusted by me? Do you envy me? Do you want me want? Tell me, why are your eyes always on me?"

"I like your style," Isaiah said, "You know how I feel about a sharp dresser."

"And how do I look with nothing on?" Tye asked.

Isaiah nearly choked on his own spit. He sat on the couch coughing, "What?"

Tye moved from his seat on the couch and mounted Isaiah, "I think you stare because you want me."

Tye knew Isaiah wanted him, Avery had already exposed that.

Isaiah pulled his hands as far as he could away from Tye's body, "Please, get off of me."

Tye grinded on Isaiah's lap, "Answer my question first."

Tye could feel Isaiah's dick growing hard. He sat down a bit harder on Isaiah's lap.

"I stare...I stare because I like how you dress," Isaiah continued to lie.

"It seems as if you like what I'm wearing today," Tye said, "Your dick sure does."

Isaiah slowly brought his hands close to Tye's body, "What's wrong with you?"

"I'm fine," Tye said.

Isaiah placed his hands against Tye's booty and inhaled deeply, "Sweet Jesus."

Tye leaned in close to Isaiah and whispered into his ear, "Why do you stare at me?"

"I sometime just like to imagine you...naked," Isaiah said in a soft voice. He ran his hands up and down Tye's booty, "I don't know why I have these feelings but I've wanted to be in you since high school. I've wanted you in my arms, on my lap, and yet you gave it all too some hood trash who exposed you and ran away leaving you to suffer. I don't hate who you are Tye. And I'm sorry for making you feel that way. But my position is important to me."

47

Tye grinded against Isaiah's dick, "And what about this position?"

Isaiah shut his eyes and leaned his head back as he continued to rub on Tye's booty, "It's perfect."

"I want you to do something for me," Tye said, "Earn my forgiveness."

Isaiah opened his eyes and stared deep into Tye's, "What is it?"

Tye pulled down his boxers in the back, allowing Isaiah to get a much closer feel of his booty, "I've made a mistake. And I've suffered through it. But my dad is still suffering, jumping through hoops to get back in the favor of the church, the church that will soon be yours. I want you to make sure my father gets back all the respect I lost him. If you do that for me, I'll never speak of this morning."

Isaiah squeezed Tye's booty, "I can do that."

"Good," Tye said as he grinded against Isaiah's dick harder.

Isaiah stretched his legs out as he started to nut in his pants, "Oh, God."

Tye stood up from Isaiah's lap to find a nut stain on his slacks, "Do you want a towel while you wait for my father?"

Isaiah lounged back on the couch looking out of his body, "Please."

Tye headed into the kitchen and grabbed Isaiah a towel. Isaiah snapped back into reality as he started to do his best to clean up the nut stain from his pant. He looked to Tye as if he wanted more from him. Isaiah started to part his lips to speak but Herbert interrupted as he rushed into the house.

"I'm here," Herbert said, "I'm sorry I'm late."

Isaiah quickly stood from the couch wiping at his nut stain, "You're fine. I just got here."

Herbert motioned at the stain on Isaiah's pants, "You spilled something?"

"A bottle of pray oil in my car came open," Isaiah said.

"You've always been clumsy," Tye poked.

Isaiah cleared his throat, "How about we talk over lunch Herbert?"

"Are you sure?" Herbert said, "I try to keep these sessions private, especially with a big name like yours."

"Nothing is private in this town," Isaiah said, "Plus, this isn't a session. I want to sit down and talk to you as a friend, see where your faith is, how you have been doing, and what more we can do to get you back in the good graces of my family. I'm buying."

"I can't allow you to do that," Herbert said, "You buy more than enough."

Isaiah laughed, "I suppose you make a good point."

"I'll make some lunch," Herbert said, "How about that?"

"I'm a fan of your cooking, you always delivered the best potluck dishes," Isaiah said, "But first...may I use the bathroom?"

"The one downstairs is still busted," Herbert said, "I might have to get the floor torn out because of all the leaking. But I'm going to go ahead and start lunch." Herbert looked to Tye, "I'm not asking you this as my son, but as my assistant, can you please show Isaiah upstairs to the bathroom."

"Yeah, come on," Tye said.

"And Tye do you want lunch also?" Herbert asked as they started upstairs.

"I'm good," Tye said.

Herbert headed in the kitchen to start working on lunch. The moment they turned into the upstairs hallway, Isaiah pushed Tye against the wall, almost knocking down a photo. He started pushing himself all over Tye and pulling down his boxers.

"What are you doing?" Tye whispered as he fought to keep his boxers up.

"I just want to taste you," Isaiah said in a low voice, "And then I'll leave you alone."

"You've already gotten more than enough," Tye said as he touched at the nut stain on Isaiah's pants.

"I've been giving the responsibility of picking the host for this year's Easter Ball," Isaiah said.

Besides the Christmas Ball, the Easter Ball was one of the church's biggest events.

"And?" Tyler questioned.

"I'll pick your father," Isaiah said, "This will solidify his place back within the church community."

"But you've already agreed to do that," Tye said.

"I know but this is something my parents will fight me on," Isaiah said, "I need more than a dry hump to give me the inspiration I need to push back against them, especially my mother."

"What do you want?" Tye asked.

Isaiah leaned in close and whispered in his ear, "I want you in my mouth."

Tye wanted to see his father back to where the man once was. He hated watching his father do silly plays and repeatedly suck up to Isaiah's parents, especially his mother. Tye stopped resisting and let Isaiah take control. Isaiah peeked down the stairwell to make sure Herbert was still busy cooking before dropping to his knees and shoving Tye's semi-hard dick into his mouth.

It was taking Tye all he had to get into this moment. But nothing about Isaiah turned him on. He was simply doing all of this for his father. Isaiah was working hard to get Tye's dick fully erect, spitting on it and jerking him off. He kept pulling Tye's dick out of his mouth to check downstairs for Herbert. Tye thought back to his moment in the sex shop with Chaz and that was able to get him hard. He basically had to push Isaiah's lips from his dick and jerk off until he was able to nut. Isaiah quickly slurped up the nut from Tye's dick.

Isaiah stood to his feet as he wiped at his face, "Am I good? Nothing is on my face, right?"

"You're good," Tye said, "If you don't believe me check while you're in the bathroom."

"I've already been up here for too long. I'll hold it in until after lunch," Isaiah rushed downstairs, "Herb, forgive me for blowing up your bathroom, man."

Herbert let out some obvious fake laughter, "All is forgiven."

Tye rolled his eyes at Isaiah's fakeness, pulled up his boxers, and headed into his room.

8 - Easter

The Easter Ball was another Riverbed event that brought together the black elite and gave them all a reason to come out and try to upstage each other. Isaiah kept his word and Herbert was the host of the event. This created a lot of buzz. Herbert was responsible for everything down to where the eggs were hidden for the children. He picked Riverbed Park near the lake to host the event. A lot of local singers were scheduled to perform, including Avery and his group. The food was being provided by Chef Bam, a young cook from Riverbed who now worked up in New York and his dishes were gaining him a lot of recognition.

At the age of twenty-one, Chef Bam had already traveled the world and had been featured in O'Magazine. Preacher Ramsey and his wife Glenda walked around the park like they were royalty. Glenda was criticizing almost every detail of the event. Herbert found himself trying to manage the event while also chatting with a mixture of politicians, lawyers, and doctors. As for Tye, who wore khaki pants, high top sneakers, and a plain white t-shirt, he was being tailed by Isaiah wherever he went.

"People are going to start talking if you keep following me," Tye said.

Isaiah laughed, "Trust me, they would be glad to see me talking to somebody like you."

"Are you trying to help me pray the gay away?" Tye asked.

"I've tried that and it doesn't work," Isaiah said, "I just want you to recognize what I have done."

Tye looked around the packed park, "I see. And?"

"Life should be getting much easier for your father," Isaiah said.

"And I paid the price," Tye said, "So...stop lingering."

"Is that how it's going to be?" Isaiah asked.

"Isaiah, we can't happen and I don't want us to happen," Tye explained, "Don't start trying to push that idea either. Everything I did for you was mainly for my dad. And you know you shouldn't be trying to get into something deeper with another guy in your position. Stop trying to make your life difficult."

"It already is difficult," Isaiah said, "People are always watching me."

"And they're always watching me," Tye said, "And judging me because of who I sleep with."

"I'm sorry about that," Isaiah said, "It doesn't mean we can't lean on each other for support."

"You don't want to lean on me, you want to be in me," Tye said, "Stop being slick and go play the good son. Enjoy it."

Isaiah nodded at Tye, "It's not my fault you got exposed. Don't take that out on me."

"Of course it's not your fault," Tye said, "But you had a great time dragging me down deeper."

Tye walked away from Isaiah not even sure if letting him touch him was worth all of this. But as he looked across the park and saw how happy his father looked as he laughed and chatted with a couple of his friends, Tye realized dealing with Isaiah was beneficial after all. He wasn't going to travel down that road with Isaiah any further though. He kept walking around the park until he bumped into somebody else who would drum up whispers and rumors because they were seen together, his father's patient, Dominique.

"How are you doing?" Dom asked as he stepped in Tye's path.

"I'm just enjoying the ball," Tye said as he tried to cut the conversation short and walk off.

"I bought my sisters out here today," Dom said as he blocked Tye's path again, "Your dad picked us all up."

"That's good," Tye said, "You know...we're not supposed to really be talking."

"Is that why you're trying to run away?" Dom asked.

"I'm not running away," Tye said, "I'm just trying to not fuck anything up."

"I like talking to you," Dom said.

"Apparently so," Tye said, "My dad told me you don't really speak to him much. Why?"

"I tell him what I feel he needs to know to help me," Dom said.

"But things would work out better if you just told him your truth," Tye said.

Dom thought about it, "I don't know about that."

Tye patted Dom on the shoulder, "You figure it all out eventually. I have to go."

Tye saw a couple of eyes looking his way as he walked away from Dominique. He didn't expect to be doing so much ducking and dodging today. He decided to simply find somewhere to sit still. Tye grabbed a spot at a bench near the lake and sat watching the water ripple in the wind. Avery's wife Shelia sat down next to him chatting away on her cellphone. She wore some jogging pants that showed off her fit body, a pink t-shirt, and running sneakers.

Tye found himself ready to dodge the wife of the man he performed for often from his room. Before he could get up, Shelia looked to him and flashed him a big smile. He once thought this woman liked him. But with the information Avery provided about her true feelings, he could truly see the fakeness of her smile.

Shelia tapped him against his thigh, "And why are you over here...too good for this party?"

"No," Tye said, "I just wanted to sit down."

Shelia brushed back her dark hair, "But I bet your momma was too good to be here, huh?"

"She's in Mexico," Tye said, "It would be impossible for her to make it."

Shelia rolled her eyes, "How could she just leave your father alone?"

"They both agreed that she could go," Tye said.

Shelia scoffed, "Your momma isn't the type to sit down and plan things with her husband."

"I don't think you know my mother then," Tye said.

But Shelia was right. His mother basically packed up and left at random for Mexico.

"I know what your father tells me," Shelia said, "And it's not nice things. But anyways, it's nice to see your father back smiling. We've been friends for a long time. We both actually grew up right in the hood together. I look out for your father. And when your mom left him and your pictures leaked, I wanted to fight somebody."

"What are you trying to say?" Tye said, feeling as if Shelia was about to punch him.

"I'm just talking," Shelia said, "How are you doing with your pretty eyes?"

Tye was sure inside she had an insult prepared for him, "I'm fine."

"Are you going to thank me for my compliment?"

"Thanks," Tye said.

Shelia pinched Tye's cheek, "There you go. Anyways, I have to go watch my man perform."

Shelia got back on her phone and she strutted away from Tye. His perception of the woman had changed so much. There was a time in his life when every compliment from her mouth meant something, but that was no longer the case. Shelia was brutal with her tongue and Tye was too guilty to come back at the woman. He was sleeping with her husband after all. At this point he was ready to leave the party. He got up from his bench and spotted the twin doctors Brian and Bryant, arriving late to the event. They were accompanied by their sister who stayed in Virginia, Kendra. And holding Kendra's hand was the man Tye sexted often, Chaz.

Tye had no idea Kendra was the girl Chaz was dating. He used to play video games with her when she would come over with her brothers to visit his father. Before Tye could dodge the awkward situation, his father spotted him and waved him over to where he stood with the twins, Kendra, and Chaz. Tye tried to keep cool during the walk over to his father. Chaz, who wore a tan suit with the top button of his white dress shirt loosened, didn't even seem bothered by Tye's presence.

Tye arrived to them, "Hey everybody."

Herbert motioned at Kendra, "Look how big Kendra has gotten."

Kendra laughed as she brushed at the bright yellow sun dress she wore, "Big?"

"I mean grown up," Herbert corrected.

Kendra smiled at Tye, "Why are you acting as if you don't know me? Give me a hug."

Tye tried to avoid all eye contact with Chaz as he hugged Kendra, "Of course I know you."

"What are you doing in Riverbed, Kendra?" Herbert asked.

54

"I'm thinking about moving back here," Kendra said. She motioned at Chaz, "With my boyfriend."

Chaz shook Herbert and Tye's hands, "Hi, I'm Chaz."

"He's in med school," Bryant blurted out.

Brian motioned at Herbert, "Chaz, this is the man that helped us from the bottom to the top."

Chaz smiled at Herbert, "I heard a lot about you sir."

"Where are you from?" Herbert asked Chaz.

"I'm from California," Chaz revealed, "My father is a plastic surgeon and my mother is his number one client."

Everybody laughed, a nervous Tye joined in a bit late.

"Welcome to Riverbed," Herbert said, "The twins are like my family which makes you family."

"Especially if I get a ring," Kendra said as she held up her fingers.

Bryant touched at his sister's arm, "You need to come say hello to Preacher Ramsey."

"Okay," Kendra said, "I'm coming. And I have to see Isaiah."

"I'll catch up with you all," Chaz said, "I need to find a bathroom," He said as he glanced over at Tye.

Tye took the hint, "It's by the parking lot where you first come in. I'll show you."

"Damn," Chaz said, "That's a serious design flaw. A sign would've been useful when we pulled in."

Kendra kissed Chaz on the cheek, "Don't whine, just hurry back. Tye, don't get him in any trouble."

"I'm the good one, you were the troublemaker," Tye said as he smirked and motioned at himself.

"Says the boy who gave me my first beer at the age of sixteen," Kendra said.

"I'll make it back safe," Chaz said as he started to walk away.

Herbert, Kendra and her brothers went in the opposite direction.

Tye caught up with Chaz, "Man, I did not know you were with Kendra."

"It doesn't matter who I am with," Chaz said, "That changes nothing."

"She's almost like family," Tye said.

"Don't get all emotional because you two used to play house together," Chaz said, "You know with this is that we have. It's not like we're going to get married or anything. You're an escape for me, from her boring ass brothers, her, and the stress of medical school. And I've told you this. Don't back out on me now. Especially because you have my dick hard as fuck right now."

Instead of the bathroom, Chaz dipped into the wooded area behind the building and Tye followed him.

Chaz grabbed Tye and pushed him against a tree, "Are we still doing this or what?"

Tye was feeling that warmth once again coming from Chaz. After all the sexting between them, he was waiting for them to finally get in some time together. Kendra was sweet, but it was not Tye's fault that woman like her and Shelia weren't in tune with the lives of the men they shared beds with.

Tye kissed Chaz dark lips, "Yeah, we're good."

Chaz unbuttoned Tye's pants and yanked them down to learn he was wearing the mesh thong he bought him. "You really like these, huh?"

"I'm wearing them for somebody," Tye said.

"You're such a good dude," Chaz said as he pulled the thong down a bit, "Turn around."

Tye turned around and looked over his shoulder as Chaz pulled out his black dick, "Be quick."

Chaz laughed as he pushed his dick into Tye's sweaty hole, "I know how to creep, okay?"

"Oh fuck," Tye moaned out as Chaz stroked deep into him.

Tye did his best to keep down his moaning as Chaz fucked him from behind. Chaz's dick was as good as he hyped it up to be when they texted. Tye only wished they were in a more proper setting than instead of the woods behind the park bathroom. Their time together limited, it wasn't long before Chaz was using his hands to pull Tye's booty cheeks apart as he nut in him. Nut oozed from Tye's hole as Chaz slowly pulled his dick out.

Chaz took out his phone and took a picture of Tye's hole, "Shit, we gotta get a room sometime."

Tye leaned against the tree upset that this was over, "Just let me know when."

Chaz put away his dick, slapped Tye on the booty, and rushed from the woods. Tye stood hugging a tree, nut oozing from his hole, half-naked and feigning for more of Chaz's black dick. He pulled back up his thong, making sure it rode up deep in between his cheeks, yanked up his pants, and returned to the Easter Ball.

9 - Chill

Tye rolled out of bed and for Avery's pleasure and just to spite Shelia, he stretched his arms out sporting some morning wood. He looked down to Avery's man cave to find the man wearing a bathrobe and waving for him to come over. Tye held up his index finger, letting the man know he needed a moment. He went to his bathroom to freshen up, slipped on the mesh thong for Perry, some basketball shorts, a t-shirt, and headed out of his room.

Tye arrived downstairs to find his father in the middle of a session with Dominque. Tears were flowing down Dom's face as Herbert sat beside him talking softly to him. Before they noticed him standing there, instead of the front door, Tye snuck out of the back. He made his way over to Avery's house via the backyard and knocked on the rear entry door. A lanky Avery answered the door with his long, hard dick, hanging out of his robe. He pulled Tye into the house and kissed him. Tye tried to pull away but Avery refused to pull his lips off of his. It took Tye slapping Avery in the dick to get him off of him.

Avery laughed as he jerked away and touched at his dick, "Man, what was that for?"

"I can't breathe," Tye said as he wiped Avery's spit from his lips, "Chill."

"I've missed you," Avery said.

"You see me naked almost every day," Tye said.

"I've missed touching you," Avery said.

Tye looked around the house, "Where's your evil wife?"

Avery laughed, "In DC. She left this morning for a conference."

"She was such a cunt to me at the Easter Ball," Tye said, "She went in on my mom."

Avery laughed, "She was in a bad mood that day. Her sisters have been being extra bitchy to her. Trust me, she's been calling me names and bringing up arguments we haven't had in years. And she even accused me of cheating on her while I was on the road." Avery grabbed Tye by the face, "But I don't have to travel far to get what I want."

"Is that why you invited me over?" Tye asked.

Avery kissed him, "You know it but I want to savor this shit. How about a Netflix and chill day?"

Tye laughed, "Okay."

"And you have to stay the night," Avery said.

"Fine, but you're going to have to feed me," Tye said.

"I got you," Avery said as he kissed Tye, "Let's go in the man cave and take those clothes off."

Tye stripped down to the mesh thong, "What are we going to do in there?"

"I want to work on some tracks," Avery said. He looked down at the mesh thong, "Are you doing that mess again for your secret friend?"

"Yeah," Tye said.

"Can we make this day about us?" Avery asked, "You can put those back on another time."

"Fine," Tye said as he stripped down nude, "Do I get a robe?"

Avery hugged Tye from behind and wrapped him in his robe, "We can share."

Tye reached back and grabbed Avery's hard dick, "Are you going to be like that all day?"

"You do this to me," Avery said as he led Tye to his man cave.

They arrived to Avery's man cave and he freed Tye from his robe. Tye got down onto the bed of pillows and lounged back. Avery grabbed his guitar and a notepad and joined Tye down on his bed. Tye watched as the man tuned up his guitar. He couldn't understand why men like Avery simply didn't come out and lived a life like this permanently instead of escaping to a fantasy world every once in a while. But he was sure the fear of being exposed...naked...was one too big to conquer for some.

"I wrote this song about you," Avery said as he placed his fingers against the guitar strings.

Tye started to laugh even before Avery played anything, "What?"

"I'm being serious," Avery said, "It's called 'Through the Window'."

Tye forced himself to keep a straight face as Avery started to sing the slow tune. He could not believe this man actually sat down and wrote a song about him. This was proof that if Avery wasn't in this situation, he could make a very romantic husband for some guy out there waiting for a mister right. Tye liked Avery, but not enough to even imagine building a real relationship with him, even if he wasn't married. Tye sat tense the entire time Avery sung to him. He was so glad when the song ended.

"How was it?" Avery asked, "I'm still working on the hook a bit."

"It was interesting," Tye said with a forced smile.

Avery put down his guitar on the floor of the room, "Come over here."

Tye scooted close to Avery and the man started to kiss him. Avery grabbed at Tye's booty as he kept on digging his tongue into his mouth. The man was definitely a good kisser and wasting all his talents on his wife and her lethal mouth. Avery slapped Tye on his ass and started to finger him.

Tye hugged his body close to Avery's, "Oh shit."

After the silent sex he had in the woods with Chaz, Tye was looking forward to getting loud with Avery. He moaned and screamed as loud as he wanted to as the man kept on kissing on his toned body and fingering him. Avery kept spitting on his hand and making sure Tye's hole stayed wet. It getting a bit hot, Avery took off his robe revealing his scrawny body.

"How about we take this upstairs?" Avery asked.

"Are you going to carry me?" Tye joked.

Avery clutched his lower back, "I legit fucked my back up mowing the backyard yesterday."

Tye laughed, "I saw you out there moving like an old ass man."

"Your time will come," Avery said, "Now let's go."

Avery and Tye didn't make it all the way up the staircase before things started to get heated. Tye stood bent over on the stairs as Avery ate his hole. He held onto the staircase banister and wall as he moaned. Avery worked his long tongue around and inside of Tye's hole. Tye grinded his hole up against Avery's face.

Avery went back to fingering him, "I can't believe this day is going to have to end."

"Stop thinking that far ahead," Tye said as he stood upright, "Where's the bed at?"

Avery smirked and led Tye to the bed he shared with his wife. Tye had no shame about crawling into Shelia's bed naked with her husband. Avery got up to grab a condom and slid it onto his dick. Tye lay angled with his head against the headboard of the bed. Avery spread his legs, crawled up on him, and stuck his dick into Tye. The bed knocked against the wall as Avery took slow strokes into Tye.

Avery looked down to Tye with a snarl, "You got some good ass you know?"

Tye was in too much ecstasy to talk at the moment. He simply nodded.

"I've been doing some thinking," Avery said, "I want to get you your own crib so I can come over whenever I want and fuck you. To me, things between us are good now but can be even better if we actually get to spend some more time together. I know I'm married and all, but it's not going to last forever." Avery stopped stroking into Tye, "What do you think?"

Tye couldn't believe Avery was doing this right now, "I like how things are. Keep fucking me."

"They can be better though," Avery said. He thought about it, "Shit, but you're right. I can't leave Shelia."

"Exactly, if you lasted this long in your marriage you want her for some reason," Tye said, "I don't get it."

Avery laughed, "She's a lot to handle but she's always been there."

"Yeah...sure...just keep fucking me," Tye said as he patted Avery on his butt.

Avery abandoned his plans to divorce his wife for a guy nearly half his age and refocused back on fucking Tye. Tye wore a big grin from ear to ear as he just lay back enjoying Avery's long dick. They ended up fucking all over the bedroom before returning to the bed. Tye lay face down, ass up, as Avery mined his hole with his dick. Avery pulled his dick out of Tye and flipped him over onto his back. He stuck his dick head in Tye's face and jerked off

60

until he busted all over his lips. Avery used the tip of his dick to paint Tye's face with his nut.

Avery rested his dick across Tye's lips, "You're beautiful."

Tye opened his mouth wide and sucked on Avery's dick, cleaning off the nut.

Avery sat on his knees fucking Tye's mouth, "And you're greedy. I like that."

Avery kept fucking Tye's mouth until he busted another nut.

Tye swallowed his nut and sat up, "I need to shower and some food."

Avery pointed to a door in the room, "That's the bathroom and I'll go fix you something."

Tye shared a kiss with Avery and went to go shower. After he was all clean they sat down for some burgers and fries. They spent the rest of the day chilling out and watching Netflix on the living room couch. It honestly felt as if Tye was in another world even though he was raised in the house next door. That night, he shared a bed with Avery. The man fucked him again before they turned in for the night. Tye was up first the next morning and left Avery sleeping peacefully. He put on his clothes and checked his phone but it was dead. Tye headed home and bumped into his father who was already up making breakfast.

"I was looking for you," Herbert said.

"Is everything okay?" Tye asked.

"I had a pretty rough day with one of my clients, Dominique," Herbert said, "His home life isn't all that pleasant and he had to make a tough choice not to be there last night. Anyways, since you were home and didn't pick up, he and I ate dinner without you. Once you didn't show up around midnight I assumed you were out doing something you didn't have any right to be doing."

Tye smirked, "Sort of, but I'm fine and didn't kill anybody."

Herbert softly laughed, "Good. But anyways, Dominque is up in your bed sleeping."

Tye wrinkled his nose, "That's not sanitary. I don't know him like that."

"Don't act like these rich niggas around us," Herbert said, "Excuse my language."

"You're fine, man," Tye said, "Is he wake?"

"I don't know," Herbert said, "Go check."

Tye nodded and headed upstairs to his bedroom. He opened his room door to find Dom still knocked out sleeping in his bed.

Pressed against the sheets he could see Dom's morning wood dick print. Tye softly laughed. Curious to see it up close, he walked over to his bed and raised the sheets to find Dom's chocolate dick hanging out the raised leg of his boxers. Dom yawned as he reached down and grabbed at his dick. Tye quickly dropped the sheets as Dom's eyes slowly opened and looked up at him. Dom let loose of his dick and sat up as he realized he was being watched.

"Your dad told me I could sleep up here," Dom explained as he yawned.

"It's okay," Tye said, "He told me to wake you up. Are you okay?"

Dom brushed his fingers through his dreaded hair, "Man, I don't know."

"Oh," Tye said, "Well, my dad is cooking downstairs."

Dom pulled back the covers and slid out of the bed adjusting his hard dick, "Can I use your bathroom?"

"I don't mind," Tye said as he tried to keep eye contact with Dom.

Dom smirked as he walked passed Tye messing around with his dick, "Thanks man."

Dom slipped into the bathroom and closed the door. Tye could only smirk. He felt as if Dom was doing everything besides slapping his dick across his face to show Tye that he wanted a bit of extra attention from him.

10 - Victim

After taking a shower Tye headed downstairs to join his father and Dom who were sitting down for breakfast. Tye did his best to pretend as if he didn't just get a good look at Dom's big dick a few moments ago. Herbert had went all out for his client, making pancakes, eggs, grits, and sausage. As they ate Tye could only wonder exactly what sort of rough day did Dom have yesterday.

"Oh," Herbert said as he set down his fork, "We've been invited to the twins' cabin."

"I thought they sold that cabin after the kitchen burnt down," Tye recalled.

"No, they did the remodeling and now they're hosting a party up their Saturday night," Herbert said.

"Why?" Tye asked, "I thought they only hosted their Fourth of July cookout up there. It's June."

"I know, but they haven't revealed any details but they want us there," Herbert said.

Tye shrugged, "I'll be there."

He was sure Chaz would be glad to hear that.

Herbert's phone started to ring. He checked the caller ID, "I have to take this."

The man rushed from the table leaving Tye and Dom alone eating.

Dom shook his head, "Man, you guys live in a different world. You're sitting at this table talking about parties and shit at cabins. Even stuff like the Easter Ball makes it seem as if where I come from is far away from this place. But the only thing separating my neighborhood from yours is a couple of stores and shit."

"Yeah, but don't let all this fancy talk get to you," Tye said, "This life is just a bunch of bullshit and misery."

"You're saying that because you don't know what tough is," Dom said.

"I'm not going to sit here and try to measure whose life is the toughest," Tye said, "But you need to remember, guys like my dad...the twins...and even the doctor next door is from the same area you live in now. They know of that tough life you're talking about even if they pretend they don't. So be careful when you say that to some people around here. Because they have as many tough stories as you do."

Dom sat back in his seat and nodded, "I guess you make a good point. It's still weird though. I mean, yesterday morning I wasn't eating a breakfast like this, in a house this nice, and around people so fucking chill. But instead I was doing my best to feed my little sisters from one pot of oatmeal. And my dad decided his selfish ass wanted what I tried to save for myself. Can you even imagine two niggas fighting in the front yard over a corner of a pot of oatmeal?"

"So that's why you're over here," Tye said, "Daddy issues?"

"Basically," Dom said, "But I have to go back. I can't leave my sisters."

"Where's your mom?" Tye asked.

Dom shrugged, "Shit, I don't know. Your mom's in Mexico, right?"

"Yeah," Tye said, "She just...needed a break from being a housewife I guess."

"I wish I could take a break from my life," Dom said, "But I have people that need me."

"Your sisters?"

"Yeah," Dom said, "Did you meet them at the Easter Ball?"

"I did my best to avoid all the kids," Tye said.

"And to avoid me," Dom said with a smirk.

"Yeah, us talking only starts the rumor mill again," Tye said, "They'll all assume you're fucking me."

Dom softly laughed, "True."

"And I'm pretty sure that's the last thing you want people to assume," Tye said with a slick smirk.

Dom rubbed at the back of his neck, "Definitely."

"Because you don't have those types of feelings...at all, right?" Tye dug.

Dom shook his head of dreads, "Nope."

"Then maybe you should be careful about who you show your dick too," Tye said.

"It wasn't like that," Dom snapped as he lowered his voice, "I was...I was...I mean, it's not like I could've hidden it anyways. You came bursting up in the room out of nowhere. Man, I swear dudes like you always got to twist situations. Having morning wood has nothing to do with wanting to fuck you, nigga."

"Relax," Tye said, "Just know some guys may take that as an invitation."

"It wasn't," Dom said, "So, get over that shit."

"Trust me, even if you were selling something I wasn't buying it," Tye said.

"And that's rude as fuck," Dom said.

Tye was confused, "I'm just going to leave this one alone."

Herbert rushed into the kitchen, "I have to go. They just admitted one of my clients into the mental facility wing down at the hospital."

"Who?" Tye asked.

"Tanisha," Herbert said, "She's one of my new clients. Um...the pregnant young lady."

"Yo," Dom said, "That's fucked up. What happened to her?"

Herbert blew out a sigh, "They're saying she tried to perform her own C-section."

Tye pushed away his plate of food, "I'm done."

Herbert rested his hand on Tye's shoulder, "Can you drop Dom off home?"

Tye looked across the table at Dom, "Yeah, I don't care. Get out of here dad, go to your client."

Herbert nodded and rushed out of the house.

"Dom, do you want to finish your food before we go?" Tye asked.

"Nah," Dom said as he stood up, "I need to get back to my sisters anyways."

"Do you want to just pack up all the leftovers for them?" Tye suggested.

"Are you sure?" Dom asked.

"Yeah, I'm not going to eat it," Tye said.

Dom nodded, "We can do that."

Tye helped Dom pack up all the leftovers before they started the drive over to where he lived. Dom sat in the passenger's seat holding the stacked plates of breakfast leftovers on his lap, quiet, and staring out the window. Tye's mind was on the Tanisha situation. It was almost depressing sometime working for his father. But the plenty of success stories, like the twins for example, also made working for the man so fulfilling.

Dom cleared his throat, "I'm sorry."

Tye looked over to him as he drove, "Why?"

"For snapping at you," Dom said, "You were right. And I tried to step back from the situation. And even after being a fucking dick head to you, you still was nice enough to look out for my sisters. This shit is just so confusing though. And I don't really know how to talk about it, not even with your dad."

"Talk about what?" Tye asked, even though he had a good idea what Dom had on his mind.

"You've always wanted to fuck with dudes, right?" Dom asked.

Tye nodded, "Yeah."

"But have you ever fucked with a dude you didn't want?"

"You mean...like a hit it and quit it type of thing?" Tye asked.

"Nah," Dom said, "Like...you always liked fucking dudes, but then one dude sort of made you do it."

"That sounds like rape," Tye said.

"But what if you sort of caused it," Dom said.

"Rape doesn't work that way," Tye said, "No victim is responsible for their own rape."

"Then why can't I believe that?" Dom asked.

Tye couldn't focus on the road. He pulled the car over near a park area, "Dom...you should really talk to my dad."

"But then he'll know about me," Dom said, "I rather tell somebody who understands what I'm going through."

"My dad is a professional at this," Tye said, "He can do more than solve daddy issues."

Dom shrugged, "Yeah, I guess. But I like you better than him."

"Is my dad not helping you?" Tye asked.

"He does," Dom said, "But I just don't really vibe with him. I don't really feel as if he'll get how to deal with the crazy shit guys like us have to go through. You've dealt with that crazy ass dudes leaking your photos and recovered. I'm sure you had to accept some of it was your fault and then move on. I want to know how to accept some of what I did was my fault also and move on."

"I got my photos leaked," Tye said, "You're sitting here talking about rape."

"But it wasn't always rape," Dom said, "Just like I'm sure you were once cool with sending that dude pics."

"Yeah," Tye said, "But what happened to me does not compare to rape. Plain and simple."

"But you have to hear the full story before you start feeling bad for me," Dom said, "Because I was at a point in my life when...I just wanted to have sex. But I never really found myself drawn to any females. I'm not dumb, I knew exactly what I wanted but was too afraid to man up and accept it. That didn't stop me from being mad flirty and shit with one of my dad's friends. I even sucked this niggas dick like three times and still tried to convince myself I wasn't really into it. And then one night, all my games and shit caught up with me, my dad's friend came by the crib and took what he wanted from me. I thought I wanted it but then after that shit was all done...I wanted to kill him."

"Dom," Tye said, "None of that was your fault."

"I shouldn't have been messing around with him in the first place though," Dom said.

"You were doing what everybody else has done, exploring your sexuality," Tye said, "But we all have our limits. If a guy starts doing something I don't want him to do, he should stop. Plain and simple. I would never forgive somebody who didn't respect my boundaries and then say it's my fault. My pictures getting leaked compared to what happened to you is a small fucking issue. It's easy to get over that, but getting raped is a different story. This man committed a crime against you. He should be in jail."

"He is," Dom said, "For stomping a dude's head in."

"I pray that he's getting raped right now," Tye said, "And I rarely pray for anything."

Dom smirked at Tye, "And that's why I talked to you. Once I heard your story, how you were abused, I figured you would get mine."

"I wasn't abused," Tye said, "I was just being a thot and got exposed to be honest."

"I'm sorry again for snapping on you and shit," Dom said.

"It's okay," Tye said, "You were just mad that I clocked you."

"So, you knew?" Dom asked.

"You barely could look me in the face and when you thought I wasn't looking your eyes were always on me," Tye said, "But I'm not mad at you. I'm a bit shocked that you decided to tell that part of your truth to me, but I still honestly think you should tell my dad. I mean...he's the father of the most known gay in Riverbed, he'll accept all of who you are and help you figure a lot of things out."

"You've reawaken this side of me," Dom said, "Like...when I saw you half-naked in the hallway...so much of those feelings I buried started to come back. Then I started trying to think of ways to tell you about how you made me feel but you made it clear that you didn't fuck with your dad's clients. It frustrated me but it didn't kill all my hopes of trying to connect with you. Shit, I even got desperate enough to flash you some dick this morning. But that didn't even work."

Tye said, "Yeah, I'm not that easy. No matter how nice your dick was."

Dom softly laughed as he rubbed at the back of his neck, "I was so nervous around you before, but after telling you all that shit, exposing myself, my naked truth I feel as if I can just say whatever to you now. Tye, it's been awhile since I've let a guy in, I've been so closed off, but simply wanting you to like me as led to me trying to share parts about myself I thought would get you invested into me."

Tye started the car and pulled off, "We can be friends, Dom. But that's it."

"Because I'm your father's client, right?"

"Exactly," Tye said, "And you need him. I'm serious about that. Tell him...everything."

Dom nodded, "I will."

After a drive through a series of projects, Tye dropped Dom off home at a crumbling house. On the porch sat three little girls with messy hair. The moment he got out of the car they ran up to him smiling and giggling. Tye could only smirk at the scene. After what Dom had told him and he saw how the family lived, Tye could not deny that they all had it tougher than him.

11 - Engagement

Tye had an endless amount of memories at the twins' cabin. He spent a lot days there hanging with Kendra and hiding from the twins in the woods to do some underage drinking. The cabin was the first property the brothers had ever purchased, always dreaming of having a place like this to themselves. The car wobbled as Tye and his father drove up a narrow dirt road that led to the cabin.

"I talked to Dom," Herbert said, "Thank you."

"For?"

"For getting him to open up to me," Herbert said, "He's an interesting case. And because of you we can now move forward. He told me a lot more about him and his father's relationship and about the issues with his sexuality that he shared with you. First, let me just say I'm proud of how you handled this situation. This is not something you can fix. His issues are one for the professionals."

"I was not going down that road with him," Tye said.

"Good," Herbert said, "But he trust you."

"He connected my exposure to his experience," Tye said, "He figured since I was hurt by another gay man, I would understand his hurt. That from one gay man to another, we could discuss the issue more freely since our minds worked similar I guess. But my shit is not as deep as his. I'm sure he'll continue to reach out to me, but I will push him in your direction at every chance."

"Can I ask you an awkward question?" Herbert asked.

"Yeah," Tye said with a smirk.

"Do you think he possibly has an attraction to you?" Herbert asked.

"I don't know," Tye lied, "I know what you're thinking. I'm not going to sleep with him."

"I wasn't thinking that at all," Herbert quickly said.

"But you were," Tye said.

Tye didn't want to stress his father out at all. He would lie to keep the man unbothered.

"He never approached me sexually and if he does, I have zero interest," Tye said, "He simply heard my story through the rumor mill and that's how he knew he could come to be as a gay man. That is all. I've got enough to deal with in my life."

Herbert looked to Tye, "Do you have a boyfriend?"

"Dad, one awkward question is enough."

"I want to know," Herbert said, "I love you son, I accept you. You can share things with me."

Tye definitely wasn't going to mention Avery or Chaz's names. And Perry was nothing close to a boyfriend.

"I'm single," Tye said, "But that doesn't mean I'm lonely. Do you have a girlfriend?"

"I'm married," Herbert said, "Too your mother. Just because she cheats I won't."

"So, still no plans for that divorce, huh?"

"Not until I'm back in the church's good graces," Herbert said.

"The Easter Ball wasn't enough?" Tye asked.

"It's never enough for those fuckers," Herbert said as they pulled into the crowded parking lot of the cabin.

On the porch of the cabin was a couple of the usual faces that roamed in the twins' social circle, Isaiah, and some of their classmates from school. Tye was not expecting Isaiah to be here tonight. Him and his father exited the car and greeted everybody on the porch. Tye purposely avoided Isaiah. It seemed as if he hurt Isaiah's feelings based on the stink eye he was receiving from him. As long as this didn't affect his father's status with the church, Tye cared little about Isaiah's hurt feelings.

Tye headed into the cabin to find more of the older crowd hanging around sipping drinks. He still had no idea what this event was about. All he knew was that they were all expected to spend the night. The cabin had more than enough room for everybody to lay out a cot or sleeping bag, and rooms upstairs for the guests closest to the twins, one of them being Tye's father. In the kitchen Kendra stood beside Chaz hugging his arm. Chaz wore a red and black flannel shirt, dark slacks, and brown boots. Tye hated how gorgeous he looked.

"Tye," Kendra exclaimed, "I was just telling Chaz about how we used to hide from my brothers to go drink beer in the woods and about our tree house we built to hide the bottles in."

"Shh, that's top secret," Tye joked.

Herbert slipped in the kitchen, "Where are the twins?"

Chaz thumbed over his shoulder, "Setting up tents out back for those who want to sleep under the stars tonight."

Herbert tugged at his waist belt, "I might as well put myself to use and go help them."

Herbert headed outside to go join the tent pitching process.

Chaz formed a smile across his handsome, dark-skinned face, "Where are you sleeping tonight Tye?"

"It's either the hardwood floors or the soft grass outside for me," Tye said.

"Be a man," Chaz said, "Claim yourself a tent."

Tye felt as if this was a special request from Chaz, not a suggestion, "I might."

Kendra kissed Chaz on the cheek, "I'm going to go make sure our room has fresh sheets."

"Okay baby," Chaz said.

Kendra headed upstairs.

Tye walked closer to Chaz, "Any idea why we've all been gathered here tonight?"

Chaz revealed a ring from his pocket, "Because I'm proposing to Kendra."

"Holy shit," Tye said.

"Yup," Chaz said, "Today marks my final day as a free man. After this, I'm done with guys like you."

Tye rolled his eyes at the comment, "Mhm."

"And I want to celebrate tonight...with you," Chaz said.

"Shouldn't you be doing that with your fiancé?"

"I'll have years of doing that with her," Chaz said, "Tonight is my last time I can fuck some ass before committing."

"Unless she's into anal," Tye joked.

"She's not," Chaz said, "Trust me. So, tonight...you get a tent, leave your shoes outside of them, and I'll know where to find you.

71

I'm going to fuck you so hard tonight, Tye. Ever since the Easter Ball I've been waiting to get back into your tight ass. You don't fucking know how good your ass was."

Tye laughed, "You're doing a pretty good job of letting me know that now though."

Kendra returned downstairs, "Boyfriend, let's go walk the trail."

Chaz looked to Tye, "Do you want to come?"

"Nah, enjoy your little romance time," Tye said.

Kendra dragged Chaz out of the cabin and off to the trail. Tye found himself alone, nobody to really chat with. He thought back to his father's question about having a boyfriend. As he looked around the house he saw a lot of couples which was making him feel like the odd man out. Two of the men he was with were in relationships and the other simply used him as a sex toy which he didn't mind. At the end of the day, he truly had nobody to call his own, but was more focused on rebuilding his father's reputation than finding love. Instead of standing around looking lonely, Tye headed about back to help pitch tents.

Later that night everybody gathered at a long dining table for dinner. Chef Bam, who was also a close friend of the twins, prepped the entire meal. Isaiah got the pleasure of sitting next to Bam and spent the entire meal brownnosing. It was clear to Tye that Isaiah had himself a new crush. All Tye knew about Bam was that even though he was famous for his cooking skills and that he once got a girl pregnant and his parents helped talk her into having an abortion so he could focus on his future in the kitchen.

Chaz clanked his fork against a glass as he stood, "Excuse me everybody."

All the chatter around the table stopped and everybody focused on Chaz.

"I would like to thank all of you for inviting me into your lives," Chaz said, "It's clear that Kendra and her brothers have plenty of friends here in Riverbed. And I'm sure you'll all also be in attendance of our wedding." There was a gasp as all eyes darted toward Kendra who sat shocked. Chaz got down on one knee beside her chair, "Kendra, will you marry me?"

Chaz revealed the ring to Kendra.

Kendra stood up from her chair as tears started to flow, "This was all planned?"

Chaz laughed, "Yeah, your brothers' helped."

Kendra looked to the twins, "I'm going to kill you two for not telling me that this was happening."

Everybody started to laugh.

"Give the man an answer," Isaiah voiced.

Kendra smacked herself against the forehead as she realized Chaz was waiting, "Well, duh. Yes."

Chaz slipped the ring on Kendra's finger, got up to kiss her and everybody started to clap. After the dinner was done, the drinks came out and the couples post engagement celebration began. Just like everybody else, Tye congratulated the happy couple. He hung around as long as he could listening to them tell stories about their relationship until he slipped out of the back and went to go claim his tent before everybody else started to call it a night.

After claiming his tent, Tye wondered if the treehouse he and Kendra put together forever ago on the ground between two trees was still intact. He headed into the dark woods and followed the trail he walked down so many days with Kendra to find what was left of the treehouse, a tattered door and a rusted barrel. Tye started to head back to his tent but heard some soft laughter.

He followed the laughter and spotted two sets of feet kicking around behind some bushes. Tye got a better view to find Isaiah and Chef Bam making out with each other on the forest ground. Isaiah had officially moved onto somebody new and Chef Bam apparently picked up some new behavior in New York. Not wanting to be involved with this in anyway, Tye snuck off and headed to his tent.

Tye was ready to get back home, missing his bed and his fan. He decided to make the best out of this moment and strip down to his mesh thong inside of his tent. Tye could only imagine how excited Perry would be to learn he slept outside in the thong. He played with himself a bit until his dick got hard in the mesh thong. Into the tent burst Chaz, nearly scaring Tye.

"You started without me?" Chaz asked.

"I was just warming up," Tye said.

"I'm supposed to be walking the trail while I call my family to inform them of my engagement," Chaz said as he unzipped his pants and pulled out his hard black dick, "I wish we had some more time but you can't win them all in life." Chaz pulled Tye's legs apart, "Keep the thong on."

Chaz adjusted the thong to get access to Tye's hole. He stroked his dick into Tye and started to fuck him.

73

"Oh shit," Tye breathed out as he dug his nails into Chaz's back.

Chaz kept hitting all the right spots which was only pissing Tye off. He wanted this moment to last much longer. Instead, Chaz was rushing to get back to his fiancé. This was a bitter sweet final fuck session for Tye. The dick was good but leaving him very soon. He did wonder how long Chaz would go before he came crawling back to him or into another man's hole. Chaz bit down on his bottom lip and threw his head back as he started to nut in Tye. He took slow strokes until he got every bit of nut out of his dick.

Chaz pulled out of Tye and put his dick away, "It's been fun."

Tye readjusted the thong, "Yeah," He said trying to hide his disappointment.

Chaz slipped out of the tent. Tye knew this moment was coming. He didn't know it would suck so bad though. But Chaz belonged to Kendra and she would get to spend hopefully plenty of years enjoying his dick. All Tye could do is sit back and wait for the next man to come into his life. Because in Riverbed, as he saw with Chef Bam, you never knew which men were secretly lusting for another.

12 - BBQ

In Riverbed as long as there was money to be spent, there was going to be an event hosted. It was almost as if these events were crucial to the local economy. The host would spend nearly thousands at the local shops for supplies and on hiring hospitality staff for the events. And those attending would spend just as much buying outfits, gifts, and renting transportation. Tye usually spent the Fourth of July at the twins' cabin, but this year since they hosted Kendra's engagement gathering they let somebody else in their social circle host a BBQ. And that lucky man was Herbert.

Leading up to the BBQ, Tye could tell things were getting better for his father. The man had been getting constant phone calls and visits from people who had previously stopped seeking his help since Tye's photos were leaked. It seemed as if Tye being on his best behavior and Herbert going above and beyond to work his way back into the elite inner circle was paying off. And not only that, Herbert was even invited by Preacher Ramsey and his wife to read a scripture at their wedding anniversary service. That basically confirmed his father's reacceptance by the church community.

Instead of being at his father's BBQ, Tye found himself listening to the event unfold outside the window of Avery's man cave. Tye lay naked on the bed of pillows on his back with Avery's tongue deep in his hole. The man's scrawny butt poked in the air as he continued eating Tye out. Tye kept his moans low. Because even though the music was loud outside, guests were constantly walking pass the window of Avery's man cave to get to Tye's father's backyard.

Avery took one long lick of Tye's hole before raising his head, "I can't live like this."

"Like what?" Tye asked.

Avery took another lick of Tye's hole, "Away from all this good ass."

"Leaving your wife for me is not a good idea," Tye said, "We discussed this."

Avery shoved his nose in Tye's hole and inhaled deeply, "I know, I know, but this is torture. I've been married for twenty years, stuck in a relationship having sex I don't enjoy. I'm a grown man and I deserve to finally be free. Yes, I'm sorry to all the women I've been with and all the children I have out there for deceiving them, but this is who I am. A man who likes licking on your ass."

"Once again, leaving your wife will not lead to us being together," Tye clarified.

"So, you don't like me?" Avery asked.

"I like you a lot," Tye said, "I've known you forever. The sex is amazing but that's all. In my head I don't see myself settling down anytime soon and especially with the man from next door. It's just not going to happen. If you're going to leave your wife and come out, don't base it on the idea of us being together. Do it for yourself."

"Turn over," Avery said as he put on a condom.

Tye did as the man told him, unsure why the conversation stopped all of a sudden, "Are you okay?"

Avery slid his dick into Tye, "I'm doing better than ever right now."

"Fuck," Tye moaned out as Avery stroked into him.

Avery kept pumping into Tye as he whispered into his ear, "It would be so perfect if we can move to New York together. I can get us a nice apartment and we can walk around all day naked. You won't have to work and I'll always be ready to feed you this long dick. That's what I see in my head."

"A fantasy," Tye said as he looked over his shoulder and kissed Avery on the lips.

Avery pressed Tye's face down into a pillow as he started to nut and groaned out, "It doesn't have to be."

The entire time Avery nutted, he kept Tye's face buried in a pillow. Tye reached the point when he was starting to have trouble breathing. Avery kept on fucking Tye and not letting his face up from the pillow. Tye used all his strength to break free from Avery and elbowed him in the face.

Avery laughed as he touched at his face and lay beside Tye, "What the fuck was that for?"

Tye gasped for air, "I couldn't breathe."

"Sorry, I was stuck deep in the fantasy," Avery tore off the filled condom, "Do you want this?"

Tye did, but he was too pissed off to enjoy it, "No."

Avery tossed the condom aside and kissed Tye, "Are you mad at me? I'm sorry."

Tye lightly pushed Avery away, "I'm fine."

"Man, we're perfect together," Avery said.

"We get along," Tye said, "But the sex is perfect except when attempted murder is involved."

Avery laughed, "So...no life in New York?"

"No," Tye said, "Go there and start your life if you want to though. Live that fantasy with somebody else."

"I should," Avery said, "But starting over at forty-five may be tough."

"You're cute, got dick for miles, and you have money," Tye said, "Trust me, you won't be single for long."

There was a knock on the door of Avery's man cave.

"Ave," Shelia said through the door, "Put on some clothes, we're going over to Herbert's."

Avery quickly sat up and in a low whisper said, "Fuck, I thought she was working."

"That's what you said," Tye said as he started grabbing his clothes.

Avery looked over to the window, "Jump out."

"Somebody will see me," Tye said, "And start asking questions."

"Ave," Shelia said as she knocked, "Did you fall asleep on that damn stupid bed?"

"Bury yourself," Avery said as he looked to Tye.

Tye started to cover himself in pillows, "This is so fucking dumb."

Avery slipped on his boxers and went to answer the door, "Sorry, I dozed off writing," Avery said with a shaky voice.

Tye was sweating bullets, praying Shelia didn't try to enter the man cave. He could only imagine the reaction she would have if she discovered him in here hiding. Knowing how much the woman disliked him, he was sure she would jump to the worst conclusion first no matter what grand lie he and Avery tried to come up with.

"Put something on," Shelia commanded, "We're going next door. You have ten minutes."

"I told you to stop setting time limits for me to do shit," Avery argued.

"Then stop being so damn slow about everything," Shelia said, "I'll be in the living room waiting."

"I'm coming," Avery said as he shut the door.

Tye raised up from under the pillows and stood up, "My heart is racing."

Avery walked over to him and kissed him, "I can't do it."

"Do what?" Tye asked.

"I can't leave her," A constipated looking Avery said as a tear rolled down his face, "I almost shit my pants."

"You and me both," Tye said.

"I made this decision a long time ago to be in this marriage and I will remain in it until death do us part," Avery said, "And I'm sorry for dragging you into this. You're honestly just a kid and should have nothing to do with the poor decisions I made at your age." Avery kissed him again, "I'm just going to tough things out with Shelia. Maybe I'll try to get her pregnant, revitalize our marriage with a baby, miracles happen for women her age."

"Please do not get her pregnant," Tye said, "She's already enough to deal with."

Avery laughed, "I'm going to miss you."

Tye narrowed his eyes at the man, "I literally live next door."

"I know," Avery said with a smirk, "I'm going to miss being intimate with you."

"All good things must come to an end," Tye said.

Avery looked over to the window in his man cave, "Can I still get strip shows?"

"If you're going to end this, let's end it all the way," Tye said, "Because watching me will only lead to you falling back into your old habits again. It's just time to go back to how things were before. You're Avery, the man who lives next door and mows is lawn at the most inappropriate times."

"I try to get it done before sunrise," Avery said with a smirk.

"Ave," Shelia shouted, "I said ten minutes!"

"Girl, I'm coming," Avery shouted from the room.

"Girl?" Shelia questioned, "Let's see if this girl sleeps with you tonight."

Avery refocused on Tye, "Just chill in here for ten minutes and leave with two sodas from the pantry. People will simply think one of us sent you over here to get them for the BBQ." Avery gave Tye a long kiss, "Shit. I'm really going to miss this. Take care of yourself Tye."

Avery slipped out of the room and Tye hung around finding himself down to only having one dick in his life, Perry's. After waiting around like Avery told him, Tye grabbed two sodas and headed over to the cookout. Kendra and Chaz were in attendance without the twins. The entire time Kendra talked about her ring and wedding details. Chaz gave Tye an almost dismissive greeting and mostly discussed football and politics with some of the other men at the cookout.

Tye headed into the house to find most of his father's clients sitting around looking like outcast like they did at most of the events he invited them too. His father's client Felicia, who had her dark hair pulled back into a short pony tail and wore an all denim outfit, brought her two sons along. They were running around the house and playing with Dominque's three little sisters. He browsed the room and did not spot Dom though. Herbert was in the kitchen and had two clients helping him prep the meat that would go out on the grill. The man opted out on hiring a staff and instead paid his clients who wanted to volunteer for the day.

Tye patted his father on the back, "Are you doing all the cooking?"

Herbert shook his head, "Avery finally showed up. He's dragging his grill over to help cook."

"Do you need me to do anything?" Tye asked.

A vase in the living room fell to the floor and broke.

Herbert blew out a heavy sigh, "Tell those kids to go outside."

Tye nodded and headed into the living room.

Felicia was doing her best to clean up the vase her sons knocked over, "I told your asses to stop running."

"Hey Felicia," Tye said, "My dad wants all the kids outside."

Felicia held pieces of the vase as she turned to Tye, "I just don't want all those people out there judging my kids."

"Man, fuck those people," Tye said, "At least you take care of your kids. They have nannies."

"Shit, I wish I had a nanny," Felicia said. "Where's the trash?"

Tye grabbed the pieces of the vase from Felicia, "I'll take care of it."

Felicia snatched her two kids, "Alright, let's go out in the back. And don't act ratchet around these people either."

Tye always hated how highly his father's clients saw the elite of Riverbed. The elite behaved like they were royalty and treated those who were in a lower income bracket like peasants. Unlike his father's clients, Tye knew these people, he knew their true stories, and they were not royalty. They just did an amazing job using their money to make it seem that way. His father's clients didn't have the money and influence to hide their truths, to cover up their flaws.

Tye went into the kitchen to toss out the pieces of the vase.

Herbert grabbed a giant pan of chicken, "I need a big favor son."

"Yeah, what is it?" Tye asked, "I'm here to help."

"Before it starts getting dark I need you to go up to the attic and grab the outside lanterns," Herbert said.

"All of them?" Tye questioned, knowing he would have to make at least three trips up into the attic.

Dom and another one of Herbert's clients walked into house carrying two bag full of fireworks.

"We got a ton of stuff," Dom said as he approached Herbert in the kitchen holding up the bag of fireworks.

Herbert nodded at him, "Perfect. Now can you help Tye get some lights from out of the attic?"

Dom sat down the fireworks on the kitchen table, "Yeah, I don't mind."

Tye dapped Dom, "Hey man. Prepare to get dusty."

Dom laughed, "I'm a man, I can handle it."

Herbert headed outside accompanied by two of his clients carrying trays of raw meat. Tye led Dom upstairs toward the attic. It took Tye a few moments to yank the jammed attic door opened before the ladder came down. Tye led Dom up the attic to be greeted by a room full of his mother's packed belongings. It took Tye a moment to collect himself, most of the furniture and things in the attic reminding him of the days when his mother was just a simple housewife.

"Are you okay?" Dom asked as he surveyed all the thing stuffed into the attic.

"Yeah," Tye said, "I was just having a flashback to my mom baking cookies and shit."

"Is this all of her stuff?" Dom asked.

"Yup," Tye said, "My dad stuffed it all up here even after saying he wouldn't."

"You guys have all of this nice shit just sitting around gathering dust," Dom said, "That's crazy."

Tye rested his hands on his hips, "And we have to find the lanterns buried somewhere in here."

"How do they look?" Dom asked.

"They're basically tall silver floor lamps," Tye said, "We plug them up out back when we host night time events."

Dom and Tye dug around and one by one started to find the lights. They would take them down into the hallway and head back up to find the others. Tye and Dom kept bumping into each other by accident and eventually they started doing it on purpose for laughs. Dom tried to climb over a stack of boxes and ended up falling backwards into Tye's arms. They lay on the floor of the attic laughing.

Tye moved to get up and ended up touching Dom's crotch by accident, "My bad."

Dom brushed back his dreads as he lay on the floor staring at Tye, "Nah you good, I don't mind."

Dom reached his hand behind Tye's head and pulled him forward into a kiss.

Tye pulled back, "Oh no, this is not happening."

Dom kissed Tye again, "I know it's not. Let's find the rest of these lamps then."

Neither of them moved from the floor. Dom moved in again for another kiss and Tye went down and rubbed at his father's client's crotch. Tye knew he needed to get up from the floor, but Dom was a really passionate kisser. Dom unzipped his jeans and pulled out his hard dick. Tye grabbed Dom's dick and slowly jerked him off as they continued to kiss. All it took was the wrong person climbing up into the attic to catch them to reverse all of the hard work Tye and his father put into rebuilding the man's reputation.

Dom grabbed a handful of Tye's ass and kissed on his neck, "I'm going to nut."

Not wanting to get their clothes stained, Tye balled up his fist around Dom's dick head. Dom started to shoot warm nut into Tye's hand. He went back to kissing Tye on the lips as his body jerked a bit. Tye pulled back from Dom and sat up holding a handful of his nut. He wiped the nut on a random box as he stood up adjusting his clothes.

Dom's dick bounced as he rose to his feet, "I'm sorry. This wasn't supposed to happen."

Tye grabbed Dom's dick and kissed him, "Let's forget about the other lanterns. We found enough."

"Yeah," Dom said as he put his dick away, "I'll start taking some of them outside."

Dom left the attic and Tye sat on a box thinking about what he had just done. He was not ever supposed to find himself in this situation again but the circumstances were different. Last time around he was the one forcing the situation, but ever since he met Dom, all the pushing was coming from his side. Dom opened himself completely to Tye, always taking the lead. And today, Dom took the lead once again and Tye hated that he wanted to follow him.

13 - Trouble

Things between Dom and Tye were kept as innocent as things could be between two horny adults. Tye knew this was nothing but trouble but set some imaginary rules to make it feel less like that. Not once did he allow Dom's dick to enter any hole on his body. But that didn't stop them from making out heavily when Dom would take bathroom breaks upstairs during his sessions with Herbert. And when Herbert would ask Tye to take Dom home that gave him a chance to jerk him off during the drive.

Dom was different from most men Tye associated himself with. He knew Dom's truth. Avery lived a double life, so did Chaz, and Perry's life on the road was still mostly a mystery no matter how many outrageous stories he told Tye. Dom was the only person Tye felt he got to know completely. And being around him was also a nice escape from the elite of Riverbed. But even though he enjoyed his time with Dom, his rules prevented him from getting the full experience. Tye had needs and right now Perry was the only man who could give him what he needed. The moment Perry was back in town, Tye found himself standing on the man's porch.

Perry opened his door dressed in his military uniform, "Are you wearing the thong?"

"Of course," Tye said.

Perry nodded over his shoulder, "Get in here."

Tye stepped into Perry's home. The man shut the door, yanked down Tye's pants, and tore the thong off of him. Perry shoved the mesh thong into his face and inhaled deeply. The man rubbed at his dick through his uniform pants as he kept on sniffing the thong. Tye was starting to feel ignored.

Tye cleared his throat, "Are you going to get naked?"

Perry shoved the thong into the front of his briefs, "I can't. I'm busy."

"Busy?" Tye questioned.

"I have to go give a speech at this high school," Perry said, "It's a last minute thing. One of the teacher's used to be in my class and I promised her I would stop by the high school whenever she needed me too. She saw me earlier today when I came into town and I agreed to do this before I leave to Germany tomorrow."

"Germany?"

"Yeah," Perry said, "I'll be over there for about two years."

"I can't believe this," Tye said.

Perry smacked him on the ass, "Pull up your pants and let's go."

"Go where?" Tye asked.

"You can ride with me to the school," Perry said, "And afterwards I'll take you somewhere nice."

Tye pulled up his pants, "I prefer if you just fuck me."

Perry laughed, "Be patient. We'll get to that. Now let's go."

Tye followed Perry out of the house upset that the man would be leaving the country for two years. He always looked forward to time with Perry and was now losing that. He went from having a crop of men too sleep with to having only one that he prohibited himself from getting too sexual with. Tye got in the car with Perry and during the entire drive the man recited his recruitment speech in his head. He cussed at himself and broke out into some road rage every time he messed up a line.

They arrived to the high school and immediately Tye wanted to leave. In high school, all he really did was follow Isaiah around and behave like his snobby friends. The entire four years of high school all he did was try to have the best sneaker game, even buying and wearing shoes he didn't like just because of the ticket price. Tye didn't break out of the mindset until he started college and realized nobody on campus cared about how much money his father made and how nice his sneakers was.

Tye sat in the crowd with the students as Perry gave a high energy speech. The man kept stressing how the military was one big brotherhood and even joked about how boot camp was responsible for his action figure body. Every time Tye took his phone out a teacher would tell him to put it away as if he was one of the students. After the assembly Perry was rushed by recruit hopefuls.

While he gave some of them generic responses and brushed them off, Tye noticed Perry gave all the handsome possible recruits all of his attention and even wrote his personal number on his business card if they wanted more advice. Tye just rolled his eyes, sure the only advice Perry was going to give one of these recruits was how to properly take dick. They left the school and Perry popped a handful of pills in his car.

"That was a lot of pills," Tye said.

Perry shrugged as he chugged two mini bottles of whiskey, "I'm fine."

"Should you even be driving?"

Perry laughed, "Stop worrying. You know me. Did you see the future recruit with the big ass?"

"I don't stare at high schoolers," Tye said.

"Oh please, everybody wants to fuck an eighteen year old," Perry said, "They stay hard for hours."

"I prefer them to be the legal drinking age and up," Tye said.

"Who popped your cherry and how old were you?" Perry asked.

His father's client King was the second guy to fuck Tye, and Perry was the third once he moved onto campus. But Tye's first fuck was the son of the actress who used to live across the street from his dad's house. Her son came home to pack up her house after she passed away and he paid Tye and his friend's some money to help. Tye's teenage hormones made it nearly impossible for him to work around the women's son.

Once his friends left, and it was just Tye and the actress' son. He ordered them a pizza to share, let Tye know he saw him looking at him, and got fucked by the actress' son in her bed. The next morning Tye wanted more, but the house across the street was cleared out and he never heard from the woman's son again.

"I was seventeen," Tye said, "And I don't even know his name."

Perry laughed, "Oh, so you were fast, huh? I bet he was older."

Tye shrugged, "I don't know his age, but he had to be in his late twenties or early thirties."

"So, it's okay for you to hook up with older men but I'm the bad guy for going after eighteen year olds?"

"You prey on them," Tye said, "I didn't understand how fucked up it was until I saw you in action."

"Young or old, I can get whoever I want," Perry said.

Perry started the car and pulled off. Tye didn't know why he held so much anger against Perry right now. Maybe because he was leaving him or maybe because he didn't like how Perry was basically shopping for new recruit booty at the high school. Perry promised to take him somewhere nice but instead they ended up at a strip club way out of town. In the middle of the day, they headed inside a strip club where a few males were dancing on stage for a small audience.

But all the strippers' attention turned to Perry as he took a ton of money out the ATM in the lobby area and started tossing around cash. Tye found himself pushed to the side while Perry drank and sniffed anything he could for hours. Perry started spanking the strippers and roughing them up. And things only got crazier after two strippers refused to have sex with Perry on the stage. The bar owner finally stepped in and kicked Perry out.

Perry wobbled over to his car, "Let's go."

"I'll drive," Tye said.

"It's my car bitch," Perry shouted at Tye, "I drive."

"You can't even stand up," Tye said.

Perry took a swing at Tye and missed, "Don't talk back to me cum bucket. You don't get to do that. All you need to do is wear what I tell you to wear and swallow what I tell you to swallow. I'm the master and you're my fucking slave. Now get in the car so I can take you back to my place and split you open. If not, I got somebody else on speed dial."

Tye kneed Perry in the crotch, "Fuck you!"

Perry dropped to the dirt parking lot and rolled around on the ground screaming, "I'm going to kill you faggot!"

Tye was done, he was not dealing with Perry anymore. He hated after so many good times, there night would have to end this way. Tye tried to snatch Perry's car keys so he could drive home, but instead Perry got up grabbing at his sore crotch and tossed the keys in some nearby woods.

"Don't touch my car," Perry said as he stumbled to the ground.

"You fucking idiot," Tye shouted.

Tye tried to go find the keys in the dark. He used the flashlight on his phone only for it to drain the battery and kill the phone. Both barred from the club, Tye had no choice but to start walking.

86

He turned to find Perry running off randomly. Tye inhaled deeply and exhaled, trying not to flip out right now. He left Perry and started walking from the deserted area outside of Riverbed. Tye borrowed the flip phone of a junky and realized he didn't even know his father's number by heart, making a phone pointless right now.

Tye made it to the hood of Riverbed and instead of risking the chance of getting robbed by continuing to walk, he went to the only person that he knew in the area, Dom. He arrived to Dom's home and looked through all the windows until he spotted Dom inside making his sister's dinner. Tye knocked on the window to get Dom's attention. The moment Dom realized it was him, he dropped everything to let Tye inside the house.

"Man, what are you doing here?" Dom asked as Tye entered the rundown home.

"It's a long story," Tye said, "I need to get to the CSU campus where my car is."

"Well you know I don't drive and all the buses don't start running until six in the morning," Dom said.

"I wonder if my dad will come get me," Tye said, "But I need his number from your phone."

"Or just chill here until the morning," Dom said.

"Man, not after the shit you've told me about your dad," Tye said.

Dom softly laughed, "He moved out two nights ago. I was going to tell your dad about this tomorrow at our session. It's just me and my sisters now."

"He just left you to look after them?" Tye asked.

"Yeah, he's living with some church bitch now," Dom said, "Trust me, things are better this way."

"How are you going to take care of three little girls?" Tye asked.

"Well, since my dad is gone he won't hog up the food stamps, your dad has hooked me up with a job doing cable installation for this guy named Larry that I start on Monday, and I got in touch with my aunt in South Carolina who's going to send them some school clothes," Dom said, "I'm not letting my dad come back up in here. We're happy."

Tye looked to the kitchen to find Dom's sisters with smiles on their faces eating dinner, "Well, can I get some water?"

Dom nodded and headed into the kitchen to fix Tye some water. Tye hung out on the couch until Dom came back with the water. He told Dom everything about Perry, from the beginning when they first met and all the way up until tonight. Tye helped Dom put his sisters to sleep and soon they found themselves in the bed that used to belong to Dom's father.

"So, you slept on the couch before?" Tye asked as he lay cuddled up to Dom.

"Yeah," Dom said, "I think the night I slept in your bed was the first time I got a good night rest in years. Either the springs in the couch were hurting me or my dad was high on whatever and trying to pick a fight with me."

"Man," Tye said.

Dom kissed Tye, "This is my first time lying in bed with another dude since that shit I told you about."

"Are you okay?" Tye said, "Is this comfortable for you?"

"I'll be even more comfortable if we were naked," Dom suggested.

Tye grabbed at Dom's dick, "You don't need to be naked to get a handjob."

"I know," Dom said, "But I've never really seen you fully naked, just some ass."

"It's funny because you're one of the very few people who hasn't seen me naked then," Tye said.

Dom bit his bottom lip as he started to strip out of his clothes. Tye joined in, stripping down completely naked. They both lay in the bed naked together, both of their dicks hard. Tye ran his hand through Dom's dreaded hair and started to kiss on him. They rolled around on the bed kissing and rubbing on each other. Tye moaned as Dom slipped a finger into his hole. Things were going too far but Tye didn't stop him. Dom took things even further as he turned Tye onto his side and slipped his dick into him from behind.

Tye grabbed a handful of sheets, "Wait, no."

Dom slowly started to pull out, "Okay, I'll stop."

"Wait," Tye said, "Just do it for a little while."

"Are you sure?" Dom asked.

Tye pushed his ass back on Dom's dick, "I'm very sure."

Dom took a few pumps into Tye before you could hear loud steps coming towards the room door.

"I left my boots and I need the EBT card," A burly man said as he burst into the room.

Dom pulled his dick out of Tye, "Dad what the fuck are you doing back in here?"

Dom's dad pulled a rusty gun out of his pocket and dived into the bed on top of his son. "Fucking faggot!"

Dom struggled with his dad as he looked over to Tye, "Run!"

Tye grabbed his clothes as Dom and his father fought on the bed. He got dressed on the porch and ran off hoping nobody saw him that would recognize his face. Tye kept running worrying about Dom back at the house. He ran until his legs barely could move anymore. By time Tye got back to his car on campus, the sun was starting to come up. After plugging his phone into the car charger and powering it back on, he drove back to Dom's house to spot a police officer on his phone talking and Dom's sisters sitting on the porch crying. Tye's phone rang and it was his father calling.

Tye tried to sound as calm as possible, "Hello?"

"Where are you?" Herbert asked in a panic.

"On my way home," Tye said.

"One of my patients have just been admitted to the hospital, Dom," Herbert said.

"Is he okay?" Tye felt as if time was moving slower as he waited for an answer.

"He was beaten badly," Herbert said, "And his father was just arrested. I called a cop I know and he's sitting at their house with Dom's sisters. I'm on the way to the hospital now. Can you please go by Dom's house and get his little sisters? I told my friend you were coming. If he takes them they'll end up being held in child social services until they can confirm Dom is okay."

"I'll do that dad and meet you at the hospital," Tye said as he turned into the driveway of Dom's home.

Tye took a moment to himself before stepping out of the car and getting the girls. If he had avoided Dom's house last night this entire situation may have been avoided. Once again he found himself in trouble with one of his dad's clients and hoped that this would not end up hurting the man's reputation.

14 - Naked

It had been a month since Dom had been attacked by his father. And all the cops knew about the night was what Dom's father had told them. The man informed them that he came home to find his son in bed with a man he did not recognize. No matter his story, the results of the beating he put on his son got him fifteen years in an out of state prison and landed Dom in a coma he had yet to awaken from.

Tye stepped out of his shower naked and walked around trying to find some clean underwear to slip on. He hadn't really been that much into life lately, feeling responsible for what had happened to Dom. He wished he could talk to his father more about the issue but that would only expose the secret affair he was having with Dom. Tye kept his mouth shut and on the outside, moved on. He slipped on some boxers and went downstairs to find his father sitting in the kitchen reading Harry Potter.

"How are you doing?" Tye asked.

"I'm on the last book," Herbert said, "And then I'll start writing mine."

"You're writing a book?" Tye asked.

"Yeah, it's a story about a courageous guy like Dom who has to fight a demon to protect his sisters," Herbert said as he set the book down on the table, "I wanted to do something to help me escape a bit but also focus on a real struggle. Many siblings out there have only each other and no help. I'm going to send half of the profits from my book down to Dom's aunt in South Carolina so she can use the money to pay for his sisters' college education."

"Is she still talking about getting Dom moved to the hospital down there?"

"Yeah," Herbert said, "She's his family, so it's her choice. They're moving him next week."

"And then life fucking goes on in Riverbed, huh?"

Herbert nodded, "Yup, we have the Christmas Ball and Chaz and Kendra's wedding too look forward too."

Tye noticed a small moving van outside in front of Avery and Shelia's house, "What's going on?"

Herbert peeked out of the blinds, "Oh, Avery's son is moving in. Shelia is pissed."

Tye took a closer look out the window to find a tall lanky guy who looked like a younger version of Avery. Shelia was helping him move in and was wearing a sour look on her face the entire time. Avery on the other hand was grinning from ear to ear as he welcomed his son into his life.

"Why is this happening?" Tye asked as he looked back to Herbert.

"I think it's a mid-life crisis," Herbert said, "Avery is trying to fix all his wrongs. He wrote checks to all the women he had kids with before marrying Shelia and I believe his son that's moving in is going to be starting at CSU this year all paid for by his long lost daddy and Shelia."

"Interesting," Tye said.

"Well, I have to get ready for a client," Herbert said as he stood up, "What are you going to do today?"

Tye realized he had no men in his life to entertain himself with, "Nothing."

He headed back upstairs and looked out his bedroom window to find Avery helping his son move everything into his man cave that seemed to be no more from this point on. Avery left the room and his son glanced over to catch Tye looking out of his blinds. He smirked at Tye and waved. Tye opened his blinds a little wider and returned the gesture. He closed his blinds, dropped his boxers to the floor, and climbed back into bed naked.

15 - Liquor

The annual Christmas Ball was being hosted at Mayor Bernie's mansion and only the elite of Riverbed were invited. Herbert's name was on that guest list and Tye was his father's plus one. Though Tye still got the side eye for his controversial past, his father was once again accepted into the arms of the Riverbed elite. It didn't take long before a stout Herbert, who wore a snug tuxedo, and thick framed glasses, was pulled away into a conversation by a lawyer friend of his.

Tye, who wore a black thermal shirt with matching jeans, sneakers, and a snapback over his buzzcut hair, grabbed a drink from the open bar. He stood with his back against the bar eyeing the packed mansion. In every corner where he looked, he spotted a man he had been intimate with. To his right he spotted Avery who was doing his best to look like a loving husband to Shelia. Avery had once again simply become the man who lived next door, keeping his interactions with Tye very PG. Over the last few months Tye actually had more conversations with the man's son than him.

At the bar Tye was joined by Chef Bam who glossed over eyes was a clear indicator of his already drunken state. Bam was of mixed complexion, his father a retired basketball player and his mother a cheerleader for the team during the man's heydays. Chef Bam had green eyes, plump pink lips, buzzcut hair that he rarely let grow out to the curly fro he used to wear in high school, and his frame was a bit thick but toned.

Bam raised his hand to the bartender as he looked to Tye, "No tuxedo?"

"Not my style," Tye said, "But you look nice though."

"My mom picked it out," Bam said, "Just like everything else in my life."

"Is that your story? Overbearing parents?" Tye asked.

"Not original enough?"

"Eh," Tye said, "But the entire chef thing is cool. I love your food."

"Everybody loves my food," Bam said, "But not enough to pay for it."

"What do you mean?" Tye asked, "I heard you were doing big things in New York."

"I peeked," Bam said, "And now I'm back in Riverbed. Letting your boyfriend suck my dick."

Tye softly laughed, "I don't have a boyfriend but I know who you are talking about."

"How do you know?"

"Because I saw you and him making out in the woods back at the twin's cabin a few months ago," Tye said.

"At the engagement party? Shit," Bam said, "And we thought we were sneaky."

"You were wrong," Tye said as he looked around the room, "Where's Isaiah anyway?"

"Georgia," Bam said, "Doing some church shit I care nothing about."

"You called him my boyfriend," Tye said, "Why?"

"Because he never stops obsessing over you," Bam said.

"Ew," Tye said, "You're ruining my joyful night."

"You're sitting at the bar," Bam said, "Like me, you're having a shitty night."

"I rather not be here," Tye said.

"I don't want to be here either," Bam said, "But I wish my food was being served."

"I thought you were the 'it' cook in town," Tye said.

"I'm working on that," Bam said.

"The level of importance in this town goes, Preacher Ramsey, Mayor Bernie, God, and then the remainder of the order is simply based on net worth," Tye said, "If you're working on becoming the 'it' chef in this town you need to be talking to one of them, not

93

me. Why are you talking to me anyways? We never talk. I didn't even know you knew my name."

Bam laughed, "We never hung out with the same people. You're old."

"I'm twenty-four," Tye said narrowing his eyes at the dig.

"A three year gap, which meant in high school you and your snobby friends didn't give a shit about the sophomore who could bake one hell of a cake," Bam said, "I don't know you, but I remember seeing you, following around Isaiah, acting like you were the cutest person in the school."

Tye remembered those days. He had wanted Isaiah so bad, "Don't remind me."

"That you were cute as fuck?" Bam questioned, "Own it. Because you still are cute."

Tye laughed, "Man, you must be really drunk right now."

"And horny," Bam said, "But don't let my mother hear that. She thinks you're toxic."

"Her too?"

"Nobody can get over your asshole being all over their timeline," Bam said, "That nut who updated your pictures must've really hated you. I mean he sat on his computer, went through your entire friend's list, every group you were in, and posted those pictures over and over. What in the hell did you do to him?"

"I stopped opening my legs," Tye said, "That's the short version."

"Shit," Bam said, "I guess you really got some good ass."

"You're flirting hard," Tye said, "Isaiah would flip out if he could hear you."

"Who cares what that dick sucker has to say?"

"A lot of people in this town," Tye said.

"Oh yeah, you're right," Bam said. He turned away from the bar and faced the room, "Sheep."

"Our friends, our family, and both you and I," Tye said, "All a part of this big herd of Riverbed."

"I thought I was above a lot of people in this room," Bam sad, "I fucking met Oprah."

"Actually, what was that experience like?" Tye asked.

"She smelled beautiful," Bam said, "And loved my food. Just like everybody else."

"I still don't understand that," Tye said, "You should own a five star restaurant."

"But I'm just a gimmick," Bam said, "I'm famous for being a young chef. The older I become, the more I become just another chef. I really need to step back, take a new avenue, write an amazing cookbook and come back as an adult chef. Until I can finish this book, I need to stay relevant. And catering every event in Riverbed can make that possible."

"How long is this book going to take?" Tye said.

Bam shrugged, "It'll be done when it's done."

Tye looked across the room to spot Bam's blonde hair mother looking as tipsy as her son, "Your mom is fucked up."

Bam laughed, "It's hard out here in Riverbed for a white girl."

"How?" Tye asked as he laughed.

"Because after being married to my father for over two decades she still thinks he has a thing for chocolate young cheerleaders," Bam said.

"Why would she think that?" Tye asked.

"I don't know," Bam said, "Because he still likes them as vanilla as her. My poor momma."

"I think you need to put down your drink and snatch hers away, because she looks like she's on the verge of twerking to Christmas music," Tye said

"Shit," Bam chugged his drink, "You're right. Nice talk. Stay cute."

"I will," Tye said.

Bam walked away to save his mother from embarrassing herself in a room full of the most important people in Riverbed. After enjoying two more drinks, he was approached by his father and Mayor Bernie. Bernie was in his mid-fifties, grey hair, big teeth, and dark skinned. Before becoming the mayor he wrote a lot of popular stage plays which made him tons of money up and down the east coast. During his original campaign he promised to make Riverbed as profitable as his plays. But the city itself was already well off but his message worked anyways and for the last decade he held the title of mayor.

Herbert motioned at Tye, "This is my son, Tye."

"I know who he is," Bernie said, "Our entire safe social networking initiative was inspired by his incident. What happened to you could've happened to anybody, Tye. We all aren't so innocent and mistakes happen. But take this advice from a man who's in the business of keeping his life private, any camera can become your worst enemy. I'm sure you know that now since your bits and pieces have been splattered all over Facebook."

Tye could not handle the awkwardness of this topic, "Dad, did you tell him about your book?"

Bernie looked to Herbert, "You're writing a book?"

"Actually, as of this morning I decided not to do so," Herbert said, "I sent out a few sample chapters to publishers and the response was poor. The book was inspired by that incident that happened a few months ago when my client was put into a coma by his father. There's a lot of suffering going on down in the hood, outside of our nice houses. Mayor, I don't want to tell you how to do your job, but that should be the main focus on your next campaign."

Bernie laughed, "I focus on what's going to help me win and those people don't vote."

"Those people?" Herbert questioned as he raised his right brow.

"You know what I mean, people in the ghetto" Bernie said, "They don't contribute to society."

"But they try," Herbert said, "It's just tough to do so when you have no support."

"I built a community center in that area," Bernie said, "I did my part."

"No disrespect mayor, but maybe you should do more," Herbert said.

"How about you focus on keeping your own household in order," Bernie hinted as he nodded toward Tye.

"As you said, everybody makes mistakes," Herbert said as he placed his hand on Tye's shoulder.

"And you're making a big one talking to me like this in my home," Bernie said, "So, I'm going to walk away and hopefully when I turn around I won't have to see your face. Don't try to play politics with me, Herbert. I'm mayor for a reason and that's because people like me and respect me. Don't lose the little of respect you've gained back by trying to take jabs at me for the baby mommas and crack dealers of Riverbed."

Bernie walked away and before Herbert could go after the man, Tye stepped before his father.

"Dad, chill," Tye said, "You need a drink."

"I can't believe he has that mindset," Herbert said.

96

"Dad, the majority of these people in this room have this mindset," Tye said, "I don't know why you're surprised the man they vote for repeatedly is the same way. But Bernie is right, don't try to start something with him especially after all we did this year to get you back on the guest list for parties like this one. You need to be out their mingling, making connections, making money, so you can someday be rich enough to help those who really need it."

Herbert nodded, "You make a good point."

"I'm going to go outside and chill in the car before I end up getting drunk," Tye said.

"You're not having the best time of your life?" Herbert sarcastically asked.

Tye playfully rolled his eyes and headed outside to sit in the car. Before he could successfully flee the party, Tye ended up running into Kendra and Chaz.

Kendra rushed forward in the violet gown she wore and hugged him, "Don't tell me you're leaving?"

"I'm just going outside to get some fresh air," Tye said.

Chaz shook Tye's hand, "You look sharp."

Tye flicked at Chaz's bowtie, "I can't touch you though, Mr. GQ. So, what's the update on the wedding?"

"I'm announcing the date to our family at the New Year's party, but as a Christmas gift to you I'll let you know that we're getting married on March 23rd," Kendra revealed, "We were going to wait until the summer but I'm ready to get down that aisle and become one with Chaz."

Chaz stood wearing a forced grin on his face, "Till death do us part."

"I'll be there," Tye said.

"At the wedding and our New Year's party?" Kendra asked.

Tye and everybody knew there was no such thing as a restful night during the holiday season in Riverbed. There was usually some type of event hosted every night during the holidays. It was expected to have a pack scheduled. Even somebody who on the bottom like Tye had plenty of events to attend, mostly for his father's sanity or because somebody like Kendra was expecting him to be there.

"Both," Tye said.

Kendra hugged him, "I'll see you then."

Kendra grabbed Chaz by the hand and dragged him off to go mingle.

Tye finally got outside and to his father's car. He cranked up the heat, leaned the passenger's seat back, and sat on his phone playing a game. There was a knock on the car window and Tye looked over to find Bam standing outside of the car. Tye opened the car door and stepped out.

"Who are you hiding from?" Bam asked as he blew into his warm hands.

"The fucked up people in there," Tye said. He raised his cellphone, "This game is more fun."

"Don't be weak," Bam said, "If I can deal with these people, you can."

"They're nice until I rub them the wrong way," Tye said, "Then they just throw my past into my face."

"Don't be ashamed," Bam said, "I told you, you look cute tonight."

Tye smirked, "Why are you hiding out here?"

Bam pulled a cigarette from his pants pocket, "Because my mom is doing cha-cha slide."

Tye laughed, "I would leave on that part too."

"Let's go back to your house," Bam said, "Let's get drunk together. I'll drive."

Tye was looking for a reason to leave the party, "And I'll lead."

They got in Bam's sports car and sped off. A tipsy Bam managed to do a decent job getting them safely to their destination. They stepped from the car and headed up to the front door of Tye's father's home. Tye entered the warm home and stood in the entry way.

Bam entered behind him and shut the door, "Where do you sleep?"

Tye pointed upstairs, "Up here."

"Cool," Bam said as he nodded.

"But we keep the drinks in the kitchen," Tye said knowing they weren't here to drink.

"I want to see your room first," Bam said.

"Why?" Tye asked with a flirtatious grin.

"I'm a big fan of interior design," Bam said with a drunken smile.

Tye didn't believe that one bit. He grabbed Bam by the hand and led him upstairs to his bedroom. They both stripped down naked and stood in the middle of the room touching at each other's bodies. Tye was in lust right now. He hadn't taken dick in a while and Bam caught him at the right time. Bam's bulging, pink dick head was calling Tye's name. Tonight was more about getting some dick, not really about the person it was attached too.

Tye got down on his knees and slipped Bam's honey colored dick into his mouth. They had no reason to rush, the night was still young and the Christmas Ball always ran late. There was no better gift for Tye than some smooth, dick in his mouth. Bam put one hand behind Tye's head as he slowly pumped his dick in and out of his mouth in the dark. He would yank his dick out of Tye's mouth and run the pink head across his lips slowly.

Bam patted Tye against the arm, "Get up."

Tye stood up from his feet and Bam started to makeout with him. They fell back onto the bed and Tye spread his legs opened as they continued to kiss. So far Bam was delivering. Bam slid his dick into Tye and started to fuck him on the edge of the bed. Tye reached and held onto Bam's plump butt as he continued to slowly stroke into him.

"How is that dick?" Bam whispered in Tye's ear.

Tye responded with a moan.

Bam smirked and strained a bit as he lifted Tye up from the bed and kept on fucking him as they stood. He placed Tye's back against his room window, messing up the blinds as he kept on stroking into him. The danger of falling backward out the window immediately forced Tye to hug his arms tighter around Bam's body. Bam took things back to the bed, flipped Tye over and fucked him doggystyle. Just when Tye was getting ready to beg for more dick, Bam pumped into him harder and deeper.

All Tye could do was moan Bam's name as if he belonged to him. Never really the relationship type, Tye was well aware of what this was. It was a drunken fuck session between two men who needed somebody for tonight. And why he wouldn't turn down the idea of being exclusive with somebody, Tye loved the adventure where his sex life took him. He loved meeting the new men that came into his life, experiencing their different styles of fucking, and getting to know the secrets they hid. Tye supposed he had a bit of Riverbed in him after all, knowledge was power and he knew so much about the men who lay with him.

Bam started to bust and quickly pulled out, "Shit, I didn't mean to do that."

Tye reached down at touched at his hole, "I'm on prep, don't panic."

Bam let out a heavy sigh as he sat on his knees in the bed, "That felt so damn good."

"Best sex I had in a while," Tye said as he sat up.

"I literally got an idea for a new recipe," Bam said, "While my dick was deep inside of you."

"Really? What kind?" Tye asked.

"You'll have to buy my book to learn that," Bam said as he slipped out of the bed and started to get dressed.

"You don't want a drink?"

"I have to get the recipe out of my head and onto my stove immediately," A fully dressed Bam said.

Bam thanked Tye with a kiss on the cheek before he rushed out of the home. Tye straightened out his blinds and went to bed for the night, naked,

16 - New Year

Tye woke up the next morning, took a shower, and headed downstairs in some sweat shorts to find the garbage sitting by the back door. This was his father's way of asking him to go dump the trash. He grabbed the bag and headed out to the side of the house to find Avery's son Spence also taking out the trash. While Spence's father was known across the nation for being a smooth operator, his son was a bit of a geek. On the outside Spence looked like a tall basketball player, but spent most of his time on his laptop, playing video games, or talking about all things geek. Tye liked his vibe though and thought everything about him was cute, from his braces to his scrawny body.

Tye put the garbage in the trash, "How was your Christmas night?"

"I gamed," Spence said as he dumped the bag of garbage he carried, "Yours?"

"I got drunk," Tye said.

"Shit, you should've invited me over then," Spence said, "But I knew you had company."

"How would you know that?"

"Don't forget, I can see your window from my room."

"You were looking through my window?" Tye questioned as he laughed in disbelief.

"I thought somebody was about to toss you out," Spence said, "But instead you were getting fucked."

"Yeah," Tye said as he awkwardly rubbed at the back of his neck, "He got sort of wild."

"You drive the guys crazy, huh?" Spence asked, staring as if he was one of them going crazy about Tye.

"You can say that," Tye said, "Is your dad still getting on your nerves?"

"And his wife," Spence said, "It's awkward as fuck being here. I'm still not connecting with him. I've been in this world for eighteen years and the first time I meet him I'm moving into his house. He's basically a stranger and there's something about him that he's holding back. I feel it and see it when he interacts with Shelia. But it's not awkward enough to send me running back to Philly. I miss home but it's nice having a dad who buys me any tech shit I need to win my love and affection. He's a mess."

"Things will get better," Tye said, "Don't give up on him."

"I'm nearly there," Spence said, "The money, the education, the gifts, are my reasons for being in Riverbed."

Tye was going to do his best not to interfere in the strained father son relationship.

"I have to put on some clothes before I catch a cold or something," Tye said, "I'll see you around."

"Alright," Spence said, "I need to go to work anyways."

Tye looked away and noticed Spence watching him a bit. Since their very first conversation he was getting a vibe that Spence had a lot more in common than looks with his father. But Avery was experienced, courageous, and a smooth talker when it came to approaching Tye. Spence's lack of social skills on the other hand seemed to keep him stuck and that lust from afar phase. Tye wasn't going to make the first move but his naughty side wouldn't mind finding out of Spence's stroke was as good as his father's.

He returned to the house to find Herbert and Avery in their running clothes, sitting down at the kitchen table for breakfast. Tye regretted not slipping on more clothes, not expecting the man he was just fucking a few months ago to be over so early. But now that his father's fight for reacceptance was over, the man was starting to settle back into his old life, catching up with his close friends like Avery.

Tye sat down at the table, "Sup Avery?"

Avery smirked at him, "Just recovering from last night. That Ball lasted longer than last year's."

"I just think we're getting to old to be out partying," Herbert said, "Why did you leave early, Tye?"

"Bam and I went to a bar instead," Tye said, "The drinks at the ball were watered down."

Herbert laughed, "I thought they were too strong."

"Another sign that we're getting too old for this partying shit," Avery added.

"When did you and Bam start hanging out?" Herbert asked.

"Never," Tye said, "Last night was fueled by us escaping that mess of a party."

"Ain't that the truth," Herbert said as he sipped his coffee and glanced out the kitchen window, "There goes Spence."

Avery looked out of the window at his son, "Yeah, he's been working at this computer shop."

"He fixed my old laptop in like two minutes," Tye said.

"He's a good kid," Avery said, "Still a stranger to me though. I've been trying to connect with him."

"You missed the last eighteen years of his life," Herbert said, "It's going to take more than a few months to get to know him. Be patient. Based on the few conversations you told me to have with him, Spence loves being here and around you. And that's all I'm going to say. Don't sit here feeling like a bad father. You're trying."

"Tell that to the other eight kids I have who aren't here," Avery said.

"Avery stop it," Herbert said, "We all make mistakes. You're trying to fix yours."

"I suppose so," Avery said, "By the way, you never finished telling me about you and Bernie."

Herbert rolled his eyes, "All I can say is I hope this is that nigga's last year in power. Excuse my language."

Tye laughed, "Yeah, when you drop the n-word you're really fed up."

"I don't even want to talk about him in my house," Herbert said, "Anyways, are you going to the twins' New Year's party?"

"Yup," Tye said, "I'm actually going out to buy an outfit. Are you two coming?"

"We're going to a separate event," Herbert said, "You're flying solo."

"Fine," Tye said, "Just know I'm using your credit card to buy my outfit then."

Tye headed upstairs and slipped on some more clothes before heading out to the mall to shop for an outfit. He kept things simply buying some dark jeans and a green and black flannel shirt. After a few nights of drinking alone in his room and binge watching reruns of the Housewives series, New Year's rolled around and once again everybody in Riverbed were slipping on their best outfits. He arrived at the twins' home to be greeted by Kendra.

"You're late," Kendra said, "And missed the wedding announcement date."

"I already knew and figured as long as I was here before New Year's I would be considered on time."

Kendra playfully slapped him on the chest, "Cute. But anyways, enjoy yourself. Drink the year away."

And Tye did just that. He grabbed a drink and sat back enjoying the party. Chaz was putting on his best, perfect future husband act. The twins and Kendra's mother showed up to the party and Chaz was dancing with her. It was rare to see the woman at these types of events. Even though her children were a part of the Riverbed elite, she still lived in the hood where she was most comfortable. She never thanked Herbert for helping her kids become who they are today, accusing the man of micro managing her parenting skills.

Bam approached Tye, "My recipe came together perfectly. Fucking you made that possible."

Tye smirked at him, "You owe me a cut of your royalty sales then.

"It's only fair," Bam said, "Let me show you something upstairs."

"What exactly do you want to show me in somebody else's house?" Tye questioned.

"Stop being difficult and come see," Bam said.

Bam and Tye snuck off to upstairs. They walked down the hallway and Bam kept turning at random door knobs until he found a dark room. He grabbed Tye by the hand, pushed him onto the bed and started to kiss all over him.

Bam kissed on Tye's neck, "I came here tonight just to see you."

"Is this what you call seeing me?" Tye asked.

"I just want to eat your ass," Bam said, "Can I do that?"

"Do it before the ball drops," Tye said as he turned on his stomach and lay across the bed.

"I need to get comfortable before I go in," Bam said as he stepped out of his pants.

Bam rubbed at his dick and smacked Tye on the butt. He pulled down Tye's pants and underwear and dug his face into his booty. Tye curved his back and arched his booty as the pleasure from Bam's tongue hit him hard. Bam made a puddle with spit in Tye's hole and slurped it up. Tye started to moan as Bam licked up and down his booty and inside of the hole. As if Bam could read his mind, he took out his dick and shoved it into Tye. Tye came here tonight to please Kendra, but was staying for Bam's dick.

"I can't resist your ass," Bam said as he fucked a moaning Tye from behind.

"Fellas," A male voice said, "You had to pick my bed?

Tye and Bam tensed up as they looked back to find one of the twins standing in the doorway holding a glass of red wine.

"Fuck," Bam said as he pulled his dick out of Tye, "It's like you can sense good sex, Brian."

Brian held his hand up, "Don't stop just because I'm here. You know how much I like to watch."

"Oh I know," Bam said as he slipped his dick back into a very confused Tye.

Brian sipped his wine as he entered the room and sat on his bed. He rubbed at Tye's ass, "It looks better in person."

"What the fuck is happening?" Tye asked.

Bam slowly stroked into him, "Brian is the naughty twin."

Brian laughed, "Am I now?"

"I've seen you do some freaky shit at the cabin," Bam said, "Don't deny it."

"Fine," Brian said, "I'm the naughty one."

Tye was shocked, once again his sex life led him into some uncharted territory.

Bam spanked Tye on the ass, "You have to invite him."

Brian stared Tye down, "But his father is almost like my father."

"He has some really good ass though," Bam said.

Brian reached under and stroked Tye's dick, "And a cute dick."

Tye eyes rolled back as his hole was being fucked and dick stroked.

"Tye," Brian said, "A couple of us guys like to get together at the cabin some weekends. I've tried to keep you distant because of the relationship with your father. But since Bam here seems to be such a big fan of yours, I'm inviting you to the cabin this weekend. It's a private party, small guest list, and you can't let anybody know you're going to be there. Deal?"

Tye nodded to the invitation, "I'm going to nut."

Brian stuck his wine glass before the head of Tye's dick. Tye moaned and hugged his hole around Bam's dick as he started to shoot nut into Brian's glass of wine. Once he had no more nut to give, Brian brought the glass to his lips and drank down the mix of nut and red wine.

Brian stood up from the bed smacking his tongue against the roof of his mouth, "Damn that was good."

The twin left the room as Bam continued to fuck Tye. Tye could not believe that had just happened. Not only did he discover Brian was the naughty twin, but that the cabin wasn't just a place for Fourth of July parties. He was definitely accepting Brian's invitation to see who else in Riverbed had a secret freak side. Bam pulled out and busted a nut all over Tye's back. Once again, Tye's New Year's started off with some dick and a jaw dropping discovery.

17 - Cabin Crew

Tye made his way up to the front door of the cabin eager to see who else was in attendance for the weekend get together. This was the same cabin Tye remember both of the twins being so excited about purchasing and that he had attended many Fourth of July's parties at. You could not tell by looking at the place that the naughty twin used it some weekends to unleash his freaky side along with a few select men from Riverbed. Tye knocked on the door of the cabin, prepared to enter it once again, but into a new world.

The front door opened and their stood Chef Bam wearing nothing but an apron.

"Sweet," Bam exclaimed as he dapped Tye, "You made it."

Bam turned away from the door and his butt jiggled as he walked across the living room of the cabin.

Tye entered the cabin and shut the door behind himself. He was greeted by the sight of two guys he knew from around town who were sitting on the couch taking turns to suck each other's dicks. Tye greeted them though they were much too busy to acknowledge him. Bam grabbed Tye by the arm and dragged him into the kitchen.

Bam sat on the kitchen counter, "Dude, strip. Relax."

Tye started to strip out of his clothes, "Where's Brian?"

Bam nodded upstairs, "He's up in his room being entertained."

"Is Isaiah here?" Tye asked, ready to leave now if the answer was yes.

"Nah," Bam said, "He's not in on this."

"Is this the usual crew?" Tye asked.

"Not really but the main crew. It started with Brian and me after we met on an app. Then we added Greg and Raymond out there. Brian met them on the CSU campus when he taught a week long medical course there. There's three other guys, one from New York who comes down sometimes that I recruited and a couple from North Carolina. They're more guys who come and go. Like Chaz, who's upstairs now." Bam hopped off the counter and approached Tye, "I've been waiting for you to get here."

Tye couldn't believe Chaz was here and a bit shocked that Isaiah wasn't.

"Why haven't Isaiah been invited in?" Tye asked.

"Brian and I usually set the tone of who can join and neither of us are attracted to him," Bam said.

"But I've seen how he's been all over you," Tye said.

Bam raised his apron revealing his big dick, "He gives me head and in return I get catering jobs. Our relationship peeks right there."

"So that's how you're working your way back to the top?" Tye asked.

Bam, his apron still raised, nodded, "Yup, The fight to stay on top never ends in Riverbed."

"I'm perfectly fine on the bottom," Tye said with a smirk.

Bam laughed as he tugged at his long dick, "I'm already feeling your tight hole around my dick."

Tye wanted to see exactly what and who Chaz was doing though, "I want to go greet Brian first."

Bam lowered his apron, "You go do that. I need to finish making lunch anyways."

Tye headed through the living room where Raymond now lay alone smoking a blunt. He headed upstairs and checked each room searching for Bam and Brian. He arrived to a door that was cracked opened and pushed into to find Bam tied down to the bed. Greg sat on Bam's dick with his dick deep inside of him while Brian used a camera to snap photos. An oiled up Brian wore a leather thong that left his hard dick hanging out in the front.

Chaz looked to Tye and smirked, "Yo!"

"Hey, I'll be downstairs," Tye said as he started to leave the room, his history with cameras not great at all.

"Wait," Brian called out, "We need you."

"For what?" Tye asked.

Brian pointed at a video camera mounted on a tripod, "I need you to get some close ups."

Tye wanted to be as far away as he could from cameras, "My hands are real shaky."

"Just grab the fucking camera before I fist you up your ass," Brian snapped.

Tye tightened his face as he went over and grabbed the camera. He picked it up and aimed at Greg and Chaz. Greg started to ride Chaz's dick hard while Brian kept on snapping photos. Tye almost felt like a professional porn director as he did his best to get shots of Chaz's black dick sliding in and out of Greg's tight, hairy, hole.

Brian leaned in close to Tye as they kept on capturing the scene, "Just look how beautiful Chaz's dick is. A nice, big, black, and strong chunk of dick. I can't stop staring at it. Life would be so wonderful if I was marrying him instead of my sister. Once, I came close to almost sucking his dick. It was down in Virginia when my brother and I first went to meet him. I snuck off to a gay bar down there and there he was, my sister's loving boyfriend. At that moment I could've done anything, anything to keep him in my control, blackmail him for dick. But, I can't betray my blood for dick. Instead, I invested in his lie. And this is how he pays me. By performing for me. You should take a ride. You look good on camera."

"I'll pass," Tye said as he processed the disturbing story.

"I'm going to nut," Chaz screamed out.

"Tye, step back and get a full shot of this," Brian ordered.

Tye stepped back and Greg threw his arms up in the air and head back as Chaz started to nut in him. Greg kept riding until he stood up on the bed. Brian ordered Tye to catch a close up of Greg dripping nut from his hole all over Chaz's stomach. Tye turned off the video camera as Greg sat down in the mess he made on Bam's stomach panting heavily. Brian looked almost obsessed as he strolled through the pictures he took. All of this left Tye speechless yet his dick was dripping precum.

Brian grabbed the camera from Tye and slipped out of the room. Greg followed him.

Chaz wiggled around on the bed, "Can you come untie me?"

Tye went over to loosen Chaz, "You never told me about this."

"It's not something I enjoy talking about," Chaz said, "Brian is fucking creepy."

"You should hear the way he talks about your dick."

"Trust me, I know. Sometimes at home he invites me to his room and just stares at my dick while he fucks himself."

"Everybody has secrets, huh?"

A freed Chaz sat up, "Everybody. So, you're fucking Bam now?"

"Yeah," Tye said, "It's nothing serious."

"Is his dick better than mine?" Chaz said as he stroked his black dick.

"He actually takes his time to fuck me," Tye said, "You were very dump and go."

"My dick is in high demand," Chaz said, "As you can see. I'm always on the go."

"Soon your dick will be owned by Kendra and her brother," Tye said, "That's fucked up."

"I'm hoping once I'm married to his sister Brian will leave me alone."

"And if he doesn't?"

Chaz licked his chocolate lips as he shrugged, "I'll figure it out."

"Lunch is ready," Bam shouted throughout the cabin, "Take the dicks out of your mouth and come eat."

Tye nodded downstairs, "Let's go eat."

Chaz leaned forward and stole a kiss from Tye. He rubbed at his body and went down to touch on Tye's hole. It had been awhile since Tye had felt Chaz's warmth. Chaz kept on kissing Tye and fingering him on the bed until Bam shouted for everybody to come eat once again.

Tye pulled back from Chaz, "We're done. Remember?"

Chaz pulled his fingers from Tye's hole and sucked on them, "Fuck. We are."

Tye got up from the bed and left Chaz sitting on the bed rubbing at his black dick.

110

18 - Taco

It didn't take long for Bam to send Tye a text inviting him over to his place. Tye pulled up to Springwater Condos in downtown Riverbed. The condos usually housed wealthy divorcees and the spoiled children of the Riverbed elite who were ready to grow up and live alone, though their parents still paid their rent. Tye preferred to do things the economical way. Instead of getting a condo, he stayed directly down the hall from his father freeloading. He was sure Bam paid his own living expenses, but based on what he knew about the chef's career that was debatable.

Tye checked in at the front desk, giving the doorman his information before he was allowed access to the building. He took an elevator with gold painted walls up to the top floor. Tye made his way off the elevator and knocked on Bam's door. A shirtless Bam answered wearing a fitted pair of yellow shorts the came way above his knees. He had his curly hair pulled back tight into a pinch size pony tail held together by a yellow rubber band.

"Hey," Bam said as he stepped aside.

Tye entered the lavish condo and immediately set eyes on the messy kitchen, "Working?"

"All day," Bam said, "Cookbooks don't write themselves."

"What are you making?"

Bam shut his door and walked over to his kitchen, "The sixty dollar taco."

111

Tye took a seat at Bam's kitchen island, "I'm fine with the twenty dollar tacos down at Mariucci's."

Bam laughed as he rolled his eyes, "As if that's any better. You said it like you eat Taco Bell."

"I'm very aware that I live a privilege lifestyle," Tye said, "I never even seen a Taco Bell."

Bam mixed some beef in a bowl, "I just got off the phone with Isaiah."

"Oh, yeah?"

"He'll be back in town soon," Bam said, "I should've recorded the call. He said a lot of nasty shit."

Tye laughed, "I'm sure he does. Are you sure you're not falling for him?"

"Never," Bam said, "Isaiah is simply my ride to the top. He actually got me my first catering job this year."

"I've gotten head from him before," Tye said, "How is he at everything else?"

"I'm telling you...he's a freak," Bam said, "That's what makes being with him tolerable. If he was just some boring dude in bed this entire situation would've been mind-numbing. When he's in me I'm cool with him. It's dealing with him out of me that drives me crazy. All he does is stress about his family, talk about you, and tries to be my therapist. I don't need a therapist, I need people to want a sixty dollar taco."

Tye still had no interest in Isaiah, no matter how good he supposedly was in bed.

"What goes in a sixty dollar taco?" Tye asked.

Bam sit the bowl down on the counter, "Everything you find in a regular taco. I just use all the expensive shit to drive the value you up. Getting the flavor right has been driving me nuts. I'm really trying to step away from the entire child prodigy image and deliver a new flavor to a more narrow audience, upper class adults. But I'm going to shut up because I'm sure you're tired of hearing about my problems."

"I don't mind," Tye said, "At least you're working towards something."

"And what are you doing?"

"I'm coasting and constantly meeting guys like you who want to sleep with me."

"Those pictures worked out in your favor then," Bam said.

"Besides almost ruining my father's career and my reputation forever, I guess they did," Tye said, "I mean I would never had become a part of the cabin crew without first being exposed. And by joining the cabin crew I've learn that Brian is really fucked up in the head. I've always seen him as Brian the doctor, who's always smiling, and saving lives. But it's been almost scary seeing how he truly acts behind all his fakeness."

"He really wants to fuck Chaz," Bam said, "You can see it in his eyes."

"Chaz is gorgeous," Tye said, "But Brian is his brother in law. It's not right."

"There's nothing really right about the world," Bam said.

"Shit, you got that right."

Bam walked over to Tye and kissed him, "And that's why fucking was invented. To make existing worth it."

"I'm starting to think you're the freaky one, not Isaiah," Tye said.

"I got a bit of freak in me too," Bam said, "I want you to fuck me. It's my turn this time."

"Shit, it's been a bit since I've topped," Tye said as he took off his shirt.

"Let me get the dust off of your dick then," Bam said as he unzipped Tye's pants.

Bam stripped Tye naked. Tye remained sitting on the stool and rested his elbows back on the kitchen island as Bam leaned over and started sucking his dick. He was looking forward to topping Bam. Forever Tye would love to take dick, but it was also nice to freshen things up a bit. Bam's head game was as good as his food. It was as if gagging turned him on. He kept pushing Tye's dick as far as he could into the back of his throat. Bam stepped back from Tye and dropped his shorts to the floor, revealing his hard dick.

Tye stood up from the stool as Bam got back down on his knees and started sucking his dick. All thoughts were out of Tye's head as he got his dick slobbed on. Bam was making a mess with his spit. He had spit running all down his face and it dripped from Tye's dick down to his. Bam jerked his own dick as he continued choking on Tye's. Being dominate right now was going straight to Tye's head, truly making him feel in full control of Bam.

Tye yanked his dick out of Bam's mouth, "Turn around and let me fuck you."

113

Bam smirked as he turned away from Tye and remained down on the floor on all fours. Tye got down on his knees behind Bam and slipped his wet dick into him. Bam started bouncing his hips, making his butt cheeks clap on Tye's dick. This was such a refreshing view for Tye, having his dick deep in somebody. He slowly started to stroke in and out of Bam. Tye kept his stroke game slow, really enjoying watching his brown dick push into Bam's pink hole. Bam's booty was really one to envy. Tye started to wonder if he looked this good getting fucked.

Bam made his booty clap harder, "Isaiah loves when I do this."

Tye did not want to talk about Isaiah.

Bam formed a grin as he kept booty clapping, "It makes him nut all the time."

Tye was no different. He pulled out and busted a nut all over Bam. Bam continued making his booty clap as it was covered with nut. Tye was impressed. All he could do was applaud as Bam kept up his stamina, his nut covered booty cheeks still clapping. Bam slowed his hip motion and looked back at his messy booty softly laughing.

"Shit," Tye breathed out.

"You did good," Bam said as he sat up on his knees.

Tye kissed Bam, "Only because I had some good booty to work with."

"Do you want to be the first to try these sixty-dollar tacos?"

Tye stood up from the floor, "If they taste like shit I'm going to be honest."

Bam crawled to his feet wiping at his booty and laughing. He washed up and they chatted mostly about high school as he cooked. As expected, he delivered big time on the tacos. Bam had good booty and cooking skills that never failed. If the child prodigy's cookbook was a flop Tye suggested he looked into booty clapping on dicks for a living. Tye left Bam's condo with his balls empty and stomach filled. He arrived back home to find his father pacing around the kitchen on the phone. Tye stood in the doorway trying to figure out exactly what the man was going on about.

"This has to happen," Herbert said into the phone, "This town deserves better."

Tye raised his right brow. It sounded like his father was about to ruffle some feathers.

"I look forward to your support," Herbert said before hanging up the phone. He looked to Tye, "I did it."

"Did what?" Tye asked as he crossed his arms.

"I'm making a big move," Herbert said, "For too long I've been trying to do things from the bottom up. I've helped many of people from all areas of Riverbed and still haven't had much of an impact on this place. So, I'm going after Bernie. I'm officially entering my name on the list for mayoral candidates. I'm going to run against Bernie and defeat him."

"No, you have to run against a bunch of mayor hopefuls first then you get to compete against Bernie," Tye said, "And let's look back into history dad. Those in the past who have tried to run against the man has had their lives ruin, been run out of Riverbed, and end up never competing directly against him because they're so damaged politically they have zero chance of winning. I get what you're trying to do but it's impossible. The primaries is a dangerous trap. That's why Bernie made up the bullshit process when he took office."

"I won't be like them," Herbert said, "I will get through the primaries and then the actual election fine."

Tye motioned at himself, "But what about me? What about mom? They're going to bring up my photos and point out her absence. I've stuck by you while you fought to recover your career because I was the one who destroyed it. But this fight you're picking now is dangerous. Bernie tolerates you, our family, let's not become his enemy."

"I'm doing this son," Herbert said, "For people like Dom. I was one of them. They need a voice."

"Fuck," Tye said, "You're really going to go forward with this, huh?"

"I just spoke to Shelia. Her and Avery told me they'll support me," Herbert said, "Are you in?"

Elections in Riverbed were dirty. So much information was dug up on candidates who attempted to unseat Bernie. The man had never lost an election in his life and Tye couldn't picture his father winning. His father's background was too riddled with easy targets like his photos being exposed on Facebook, his mother being all the way in Mexico instead of at home with her husband, and he was sure Bernie would convince some clients to turn against Herbert. Tye could only imagine what else would come to light, like the cabin crew, his time with Avery, anything. But he couldn't leave his father hanging.

"You are walking us to our graves," Tye said, "But fuck it, you have my support."

Herbert hugged Tye, "We can win this son."

Tye wanted to believe that. He was trying hard to do so. It wasn't working.

19 - Mexico

Along with his father, six others were competing in the primaries for a chance to face Bernie. This entire primaries system was put in place by Bernie just to give his team more than enough time to attack and destroy each person who wished to face him one by one. Originally there were seven candidates competing against Herbert in the primaries. But one immediately dropped out after it was leaked that he had contracted a STD two months ago. This was the petty stuff Bernie did to tear down his competition. Tye was nervous for his father.

He sat in the kitchen watching Herbert, Shelia, and Avery trying to put together a list of the people Herbert needed to have in his corner to win this election. Tye told his father he would support him but really wasn't into the entire idea. It made him nervous knowing right now one of Bernie's staffers was out in Riverbed digging up dirt on him, his father, and mother.

"You need the church," Shelia said.

Avery kissed his wife on the cheek, "Good call."

Herbert nodded, "I'll talk to Isaiah. He likes me more than his parents."

Shelia looked back to Tye, "You were friends with Isaiah, right?"

"In high school, sort of," Tye said.

"Are you still friends with him or what?" Shelia asked with an attitude.

Tye could not believe he was so blind to her hatred towards him, "Sort of."

Shelia scoffed and rolled her eyes, "Maybe you should just do coffee runs. You're working against us."

Tye wished he could toss some coffee in her face.

Avery rubbed at his wife's back, "If you start stressing I'll start stressing."

"I'm fine," Shelia said as she knocked Avery's hand away, "I just hate unproductive people."

"We are all doing good so far," Herbert said. He looked to Tye, "I'll talk to Isaiah, okay?"

"Okay," Tye said staring a hole into the back of Shelia's head of flowing dark hair.

Shelia looked back at Tye as if she could feel him staring her down, "Spence was working on the posters."

"Okay?"

"Go check on them Tye," Shelia snapped as if he could read her mind, "I mean...do something. Move it, boy."

Herbert softly chuckled, "The intensity of this is getting to us all. Let's not crack."

"I'm good," Tye said, "I'm not cracking at all."

"Tye," Shelia called out, "The posters? Spence? Go."

Tye rolled his eyes as he headed over next door. Tye was always aware at how iffy things were between Shelia and his mother, but never realized how harsh she was towards him. He simply thought Shelia was an aggressive person. But saw it simply as her having a stink attitude, especially towards him. Tye knocked on Shelia and Avery's house door and Spence answered carrying a laptop in his hand and listening to some headphones. He wore some bright red boxers, white ankle socks, and a black tank-top.

He lowered his headphones and smirked, revealing his mouthful of braces, "You okay?"

"Is Shelia a bitch to you also?"

"Yeah, but she mostly ignores me," Spence said, "I like being off her radar. What's up?"

"They sent me over here to look at the posters."

Spence nodded over his shoulder, "I'm glad you came over."

"I don't care how they look honestly," Tye said, "This campaign is suicide."

Spence shut the door, "Is it because of these?"

He faced the laptop screen towards Tye revealing his leaked photos.

"Why in the fuck do you have those?" Tye questioned.

"This is my dad's laptop," Spence said, "I was using mine to download some torrents and it was slowing down publisher. So, I grabbed his and this fool didn't even have a password for his user account. I was searching around for the publisher execution icon and accidentally clicked on this folder that has these photos and these."

Spence hit play a button and a video of Tye stripping for Avery across in his room played.

"Fuck," Tye said.

Spence closed the video, "At first I thought he was spying. But it looked like you were performing."

"I did not know he recorded those," Tye said, "Or that he still had those pictures."

Spence sat down on the couch, "What the fuck is going on between you two?"

"Nothing at all," Tye said, "Delete those videos."

"He'll notice that they're gone and that'll fuck up my entire situation here," Spence said, "This isn't my most favorite place to be but I'm getting used to it. It's nice going to a college that actually teaches me shit, I like my job at the shop, my dad is still a fucking stranger to me, but I can't complain really."

Tye sat down next to Spence, "I can't believe he recorded me."

"You can't sit here and tell me nothing was happening between you two," Spence said, "You're gay and strip for my dad. Which means he's also gay, right?"

"He's...Avery," Tye said, "You talk to him about that."

"Have you been sleeping with him?" Spence asked.

"No," Tye said.

"I mean...have you ever slept with him?" Spence asked.

"Why does it even matter?"

Spence shrugged, "I think it's funny. And I want to be in on something. I feel so excluded in this town."

"You don't want to be included in any Riverbed weirdness," Tye said, "Focus on work and school."

"You had sex with my dad," Spence said as he softly laughed, "Damn. Poor Shelia."

"Fuck Shelia," Tye said.

"You're bad, Tye," Spence said as he kept laughing, "And yet guys like me get a bad rep."

"Huh?"

"You come off like the innocent rich boy from a nice town," Spence said, "While guys like me from Philly...the urban jungle...the hood...get the bad reps. I work and focus on school. You're the one going around sleeping with married men and getting banged out against your bedroom window. I knew you were bad but not this bad."

"Then you're late to the party," Tye said, "Those pictures killed my innocent act. Exposed all of me."

Spence sat the laptop on the table, "Those pictures were sexy as hell though."

Tye almost expected this conversation to come, "Shit, you too, huh?"

"Me, what?"

"Since those pictures leaked...guys have just been falling into my lap," Tye said.

Spence laughed, "I would rather fall into your ass, but yeah...you make my dick hard."

Tye laughed, "Yea, whatever. Join the club."

"So, are you done fucking my dad?"

"Yeah, since months ago," Tye said.

"So, you're single?" Spence asked as he bit his bottom lip.

"I've always been single," Tye said.

"We get along, right?"

"You're cool," Tye said, "But I'm not going to sleep with you."

"What?" Spence whined, "Why not?"

"Because I just don't sleep with guys because they like my pictures," Tye said, "I can't go from fucking your dad to fooling around with you. You're some eighteen year old kid who's all turned on by a nude picture and you think just because the entire town has seem my asshole that it's open for business."

"Oh, so I'm a kid now?"

"You know what I mean," Tye said, "When I was eighteen I was just a dumb kid."

Spence pulled his long, skinny, dick, out of his boxers, "I'm all man."

It was clear Spence was Avery's son. He had a long dick just like his father, possibly even longer. Tye just sat there rolling his eyes on the inside as Spence ran his tongue across his braces and slapped his dick from side to side. Tye knew by the way Spence stared at him sometime that he wanted him. And Tye had already decided multiple times that he would not lay a hand on Spence period. But he thought he was cute: tall, lean, nice brown lips. His entire geek vibe was working for him. And most importantly, his dick was a hit with Tye's hormones right now.

Tye reached out and gripped Spence's dick, "Damn."

Spence breathed heavily, "Are we about to do this? Should we go in the room? Oh, fuck."

"Are you a virgin?" Tye asked as he slowly slid his hand down Spence's dick, "Don't lie."

Spence nodded, "Yeah. Let's go in my room before somebody walks in."

Tye could tell by the way Spence's dick was pulsating this was almost already over, "We're good right here."

Tye slowly slid his hand up Spence's dick and back down. Spence grabbed onto the couch cushions and two simple strokes of his long dick was enough to get him to start shooting nut out like a water gun. Tye kept stroking Spence's dick slow and nut flew all over his shirt. Nut drained all down Spence's dick and got all over Tye's hand.

Spence was nearly in tears as he sat back convulsing, "Fuck. Fuck."

Tye removed his hand away from Spence's dick and started to lick it clean.

"Oh shit," Spence said, "You're gonna eat my nut?"

Tye laughed as he licked his fingers clean, "Yeah."

"Do you like it?" Spence asked as he looked down at the mess he made all over himself.

Tye stood up from the couch, "Yeah, it was good."

"Do I have to jerk you off now?"

"You're good," Tye said, "Just clean yourself up and finish those posters."

Spence's dick dripped nut as he slowly stood up, "Thank you."

"No, problem," Tye said as he grabbed Spence's dick, "Next time I might give you some head."

Spence's knees went weak as Tye played with his dick, "Fuck. I'm down."

Tye smirked at him and left the house. He arrived outside to find a muscled hispanic man wearing fitted green shorts and a white dress shirt unloading bags from the back of a taxi. Out of the back seat of a taxi stepped a woman with stylish, curly, low cut dark hair and wearing a flowered pattern cocktail dress with white heels. Tye could not believe this. His mother was back. Jolie made her way over to the hispanic man and kissed him on the lips before spotting her son standing outside of Shelia and Avery's house.

Jolie shrieked, "Tye!"

Tye sped walk over to his mother and hugged her, "Yo, what are you doing here?"

Jolie stepped back from her son, "Your father called."

"Is this your son?" The hispanic man interrupted with a thick accent.

"Yes, Rodriguez," Jolie said, "This is my one and only, Tye."

Rodriguez shook Tye's hand, "Nice to meet you," He said before walking off to go pay the taxi driver.

"Mom, is that your boyfriend?" Tye asked, already knowing the answer.

"Yes," Jolie proudly said, "He taught me Spanish. I don't remember most of it. But yeah. That's my man."

"And you brought him with you because dad called...your husband?" Tye questioned.

Jolie kissed him on the forehead, "Yes. I heard he's running against Bernie and needs me at his side."

"And you came all the way from Mexico just because of that?"

Jolie nodded, "I always told your father if he really needed me I would come. And plus, I missed you."

Tye's mother hugged him again. He looked over her shoulder at Rodriguez whose dick print was very obvious in his fitted shorts. He completely understood why she didn't leave him behind in Mexico. But all Tye could wonder was how the presence of his mother's boyfriend would make this campaign even more difficult to keep from derailing.

20 - Let Me

The moment Jolie stepped into the home with Rodriguez trailing behind her the mood changed. All the campaign planning and panic went away. You could tell by the look on Herbert's face that he didn't know if he should go hug his wife or punch out her boyfriend. Avery was clearly struggling not to stare at Rodriguez too hard. And Shelia, she couldn't force herself to pretend she was happy to see Jolie.

Jolie adjusted her dress a bit as she joined them in the kitchen, "Well, hi."

"I'm glad you made it," Herbert said.

"It's nice seeing you Jolie," Avery added.

"I'm going to head home," Shelia said as she avoided eye contact with Jolie. "Oh, and nice seeing you Jo."

Jolie softly laughed, "Bye. I guess we'll catch up another time."

Shelia grabbed her purse and Avery by the arm and basically dragged the man out of the home.

"Where's the restroom?" Rodriguez asked.

Tye pointed upstairs, "To your left, first door."

Rodriguez nodded and headed upstairs.

Jolie rested her hands on her hips as she surveyed the kitchen, "You changed everything."

"I know," Herbert said, "It was all getting stale."

"And did you just toss my belongings in the garbage?" Jolie asked.

"I put them all up in the attic."

"You promised you weren't going to do that," Jolie said.

"And you promised you would come back," Herbert said, "I had to call you back."

"You're right," Jolie said, "It feels so odd being back in the suburbs. My apartment back in Mexico is the size of this kitchen. It's a nice apartment though. I miss it here though. Being a mom. Being a wife. I'm looking forward into getting back into that role."

"It's not a role," Herbert said, "You are a wife and a mom. Don't say that in front of the press, ever."

Jolie nodded, "Gotcha." She looked to Tye, "Do you think he can beat Bernie?"

Tye didn't want to be mister negative, "Um, do you think he can beat Bernie?"

Jolie looked to Herbert and smirked, "Of course he can. And apparently Shelia and Avery believes in him also."

Herbert started to clean up the kitchen, "One of Avery's sons is living with them now."

"Wow," Jolie said, "What else has changed around here?"

"Kendra is getting married and Isaiah is getting one step closer to taking over his father's church," Herbert said.

"Have you talked to Isaiah?" Jolie asked, "You need his support, the church."

"I'll make sure I talk to him," Herbert said, "We're close again. Even after Facebook-gate."

Jolie looked to Tye as she laughed, "I thought you looked very handsome in your pictures."

An embarrassed Tye rolled his eyes, "Mom. Don't."

"I've seen you naked plenty of times before," Jolie said.

"Yeah, when I was a baby," Tye said, "Not a grown man."

"You're still as smooth as you were as a baby though," Jolie poked.

"I'm going to sleep," Tye said as he tried not to laugh.

Tye made his way upstairs as Rodriguez and his flopping bulge was coming downstairs. He simply smirked and nodded at the man before heading into his bedroom, stripping naked, and getting into bed. The next morning he woke up to the sound of muffled voices and stomping over his head. He rolled out of bed, slipped on some shorts and peeked out of his bedroom to find Rodriguez wearing some yellow briefs and carrying a box from the attic. Jolie made her way down behind her boyfriend wearing a white sundress and flip flops.

"Mom, what are you doing?" Tye asked.

"Making myself feel back at home," Jolie said, "We're the perfect family again, right?"

"Yeah, I guess."

"So, I'm putting some of my items around the house to make it feel just like home again," Jolie said.

"And I'm helping," Rodriguez said.

Jolie kissed Rodriguez, "You're so damn helpful."

Tye still could not believe she brought her boyfriend. He slipped out of his bedroom and left them to their makeout session. Tye arrived to find his father downstairs sitting at the cluttered kitchen table working hard to put his campaign together. The man was taking phone calls and sending emails all at the same time.

Tye joined his father at the table, "So, she brought her boyfriend."

"It was a part of the deal," Herbert said, "She didn't want to travel alone."

"Are you going to push for that divorce now?"

"It's going to happen," Herbert said, "But not anytime soon. It'll ruin my campaign. Do you think I can win?"

"Stop asking me that," Tye said, "You have my support."

"But do I have your confidence in me?"

"Dad, Bernie has already ruined one candidate. How long before he comes after you and us?" Tye worried.

"If he comes for me, I'll come for him," Herbert said, "Riverbed needs a mayor that cares about all, not just the rich."

"Aka people like you, me, our friends."

"That doesn't mean I can't help those in need, the ignored, you know that," Herbert said, "I'm going to win."

"And I'm going to shower," Tye said.

Tye headed back upstairs to find Jolie and her boyfriend bringing down more boxes. He took a shower and checked his phone to learn he had a text from Bam. Tye was being invited to Chaz's secret bachelor party tonight at the cabin. He had to decide between being around a bunch of good looking men or helping his father come up with a campaign slogan. Tye clearly was going to hit up the bachelors party.

Jolie poked her head into his room and tossed him a credit card, "Go buy groceries."

"Why?" Tye asked as he caught the card.

"Because Herbert is busy, Rodriguez doesn't exist, and I'm redecorating," Jolie said, "I plan on cooking dinner five days a week until this election is won. And plus the refrigerator is empty. So, take my card and go buy everything. There's no limit so don't be cheap."

"Mom, how exactly do you make money in the Peace Corp?" Tye asked.

"I survive," Jolie said, "But Roddy's family manufactures cigarettes. So that should answer your question."

"Gotcha," Tye said as he slipped the card into his pocket, "I'll head out now."

Tye slipped on some khaki slacks, a red long sleeved shirt, and went over to Pam's super store where everything was sold in bulk. He found himself pushing an extra wide buggy, tossing anything he could grab into the cart. Tye did his best to try to remember which foods his mom made the best and got all the ingredients she would need. He turned onto the frozen foods aisle and nearly ran over the last person he wanted to see. Before him, stood Isaiah wearing black slacks, a white dress shirt, and a yellow sweater vest.

Isaiah's face lit up, "What are you doing here?"

"Grocery shopping," Tye said as he motioned at the buggy full of food, "Clearly."

Isaiah laughed, "Of course. I'm a bit tired. I just got back in town. I was in Georgia."

"That's good, but I need to go check out."

"Wait," Isaiah said, "I had a dream about you. Heck, I can't even talk about it out in the open."

"Oh, okay," Tye said as he tried to push his buggy around Isaiah who kept blocking his path.

"You look good, Tye," Isaiah complimented, "We have to start spending more time together."

"For the sake of your reputation, as I said before, no," Tye said, "You're a future pastor, I'm a thot."

"You're not a thot," Isaiah said as he softly laugh, "Or whatever that is."

"A thot has nude pictures on Facebook...a thot sat on your lap- "

"-I get it," Isaiah said, cutting Tye's words short.

"Bye Isaiah," Tye said as he managed to push pass him.

Though Tye wasn't done shopping, he didn't want to bump into Isaiah again. He went to checkout and headed back home to find his mom still redecorating and his father still working on his campaign now with the help of Avery. Tye loaded all the groceries and hung out around the house asking his mom a barrage of questions about life down in Mexico before he headed out to the cabin bachelor party. He arrived at the cabin and Brian answered the door wearing a leather choker around his neck and a red cockring on his swollen dick and balls.

Brian smirked, "Strip."

"Can I come in first?"

"I said strip," Brian commanded.

Tye could not believe he was always so blind to Brian's kinkiness. He stripped out of his clothes on the porch and passed them to Brian. Brian tossed them in a basket near the door before allowing Tye to enter. Tye entered the cabin to find a nude Bam and Chaz hanging out on the couch and a couple of empty beer bottles on the coffee table. His dick got hard the moment he set eyes on Chaz's chocolate dick and Bam's thick booty.

"Sup?" Tye said as he joined them on the couch.

"I'm catering the wedding," Bam beamed, "Chaz just confirmed it."

Brian made his way over to him, "Hold up, did Tye just say sup?"

Tye nodded, "Yeah, what's wrong with that."

"We don't greet each other like that in here," Brian said, "Bam, greet Tye."

Bam grabbed Tye and planted a sloppy kiss on his lips, "That's how we greet."

Brian leaned forward and also shared a kiss with Tye, "That's how we say what's up. Chaz, greet him."

Chaz hesitated a bit before scooting close to Tye and kissing him. Unlike with Brian and Bam, Tye still felt that warmth he got from Chaz every time they touched. Their kiss was turning into a full blown makeout session. Tye realized both Bam and Brian were staring them down. He pulled back from Chaz.

"I hope you kiss my sister like that on your wedding night," Brian said, "That was intense. You two fucked?"

"No," Bam lied, "You're the first one to take advantage of my situation."

"Don't say it like that," Brian said, "You caused this on yourself. Dating my sister while fooling around with men."

"I was going to stop eventually," Chaz said.

"We never stop fucking what we want," Brian said, "I need a beer."

Bam stood up from the couch, "Me too. I'm coming with you."

They both left the living room.

Tye looked to Chaz, "So, he doesn't know about us?"

"Hell no," Chaz said, "Brian is a jealous bitch. I don't want him coming after you."

"Well, are you okay?"

"Besides the fact that my brother in law wants me bad, I'm fine. I want this wedding to be over with and done."

"Do you really want to marry Kendra?" Tye asked.

"I was feeling alright about it until psycho brother came around," Chaz said.

"Who else is here tonight?" Tye asked.

"Just us," Chaz said.

"Well, then who's fucking who?" Tye asked.

It wasn't long before that question was answered. After a couple of beers all four of them headed upstairs. Both Tye and Bam found themselves playing the role of the bottoms. Brian and Chaz lay back in the bed as they both got head. Bam sucked Chaz's dick while Tye got to suck on Brian's oiled up slug of a dick. Tye had zero interest in Brian. He was more focused on watching Chaz get head. All Tye could think about was kissing on Chaz's dark chocolate body, feeling his warmth.

They switched positions and Bam and Tye found themselves making out as they were fucked from behind. Bam was making his booty clap as Chaz fucked him fast. While Tye's hole was being filled up with Brian's dick and being treated to his slow stroke. Once again, all of Tye's focus was on Chaz. Wishing it was him taking his dick instead of Bam. Brian pulled out of Tye, crawled into the center of the bed and arched his booty.

He rubbed at his hole, "It's my turned to get fucked."

"Okay," Tye said.

Brian pushed Tye away, "Not by you. Chaz, fuck me."

Chaz kept fucking Bam, "Stop playing."

"Get over here and fuck me," Brian demanded.

Chaz pulled out of Bam, "You're my brother in law. You know we don't ever touch."

"I don't care what we are or about to become, it's just fucking," Brian said, "Fuck me!"

Chaz shook his head at Brian in disgust and left the room.

Brian cussed under his breath. He looked to Bam, "Well, can you be a man and fuck me?"

Bam nodded as he started to work on slipping his dick into Brian. Tye wanted to go check on Chaz. But as Brian started to get fucked, he reached for Tye's dick and started to pull it towards his mouth. Brian took Bam's dick and sucked Tye's dick at the same time. Tye didn't care about any of this. He just wanted to make sure Chaz was okay.

21 - Manners

It took one simple text to sum up how Chaz was doing. He simply had replied to Tye 'I'm fine. Fuck Brian'. Tye could only wonder how Brian and Chaz's strained relationship would affect the wedding. He didn't want Kendra to get hurt, but Tye saw himself as a part of the problem. If he had truly cared about Kendra's feelings he would've never slept with Chaz and tell her about the craziness going on between her brother and future husband. Tye simply stepped away from the drama and got in some mommy and son time. While Avery was inside helping Herbert with the campaign, Tye hung out with his mom in the backyard in the grass. They both sat enjoying the early spring weather watching Rodriguez do some push-ups.

"He never skips a workout," Jolie said, "Back at home, he does it without his clothes."

Tye simply laughed, "Do you love him?"

"I'm a bit confused about what love is right now," Jolie said, "I love his company."

"But you loved dad?"

"Back then I did," Jolie said, "Until he became so damn boring. You kept things fun though."

"Is that why you had me?"

"No, we wanted five kids," Jolie said, "Instead we got an amazing one."

"It's nice being complimented, it's rare for me," Tye said.

"Oh don't lie," Jolie said, "I'm sure the boys have just been crawling all over you. To be honest, I'm afraid to ask who you've been messing around with. The men of Riverbed think we women are blind, but we know so much about what they do on these ski trips and business trips they go on. I always knew Herbert was one hundred percent straight though. He's too boring to suck a dick."

"Damn mom, get a filter," Tye said as he laughed.

"You're twenty-four, you've heard that word before," Jolie said, "So, who are you sleeping with?"

"None of your business."

"Tell me one and I'll bake some cookies tonight."

Tye really liked his mother's baking. He decided to give up a name that would cause the least drama, "Perry."

"Perry? Out of all the men in Riverbed you throw out a name I don't know. Cheater. Who is he?"

"A professor, army guy, psycho path," Tye said, "He left for Germany."

"So, you like older men?"

"I like men in general," Tye said.

"Did you love Perry?"

"Oh fuck no," Tye said.

"Have you ever loved somebody?" Jolie asked.

"Not yet," Tye said.

"Name a guy out there right now that you can't get off your mind," Jolie said, "Please."

"You can't say anything," Tye said.

"Boy, stop it, I don't even socialize with anybody in Riverbed anymore."

"Chaz."

Jolie laughed, "Another name I don't know."

"He's marrying Kendra."

Jolie gasped, "Son."

"I know," Tye said, "It's dangerous territory. He's just on my mind because of some mess he's going through that I happen to be very aware of. As a friend, I feel bad for him."

"Do you get vibes from him?"

"None at all. I've barely shaken his hand," Tye lied.

"Don't ruin that girl's marriage," Jolie said, "Leave that up to her and Chaz."

"Do you feel as if you've ruined your marriage with dad? For example, bringing Roddy here with you?"

"I ruined it the day I left," Jolie said, "No good wife leaves her husband for anything. Me coming back now is just my way of saying sorry. I really want him to become mayor of this town. He's a good man. Bernie is a piece of shit. And in a way I'll feel as if he'll like me more because I helped play a part in his victory. He's still sweet to me now, but something is different. Do you think Shelia puts things in his head about me?"

"I think Shelia puts things in his head about the both of us," Tye said, "She's been a bitch to me."

"Son, she's always been a bitch. You were just too young to realize that," Jolie said, "But she knows that she can't take things too far with me. Because unlike you, I can hit her. And I will. So far she's been hiding since I've come back but I know she's going to try to come for me. I don't know how or when, but it's going to happen."

A sweaty Rodriguez walked over to them, "How about a shower?"

Jolie got up and kissed Rodriguez, "I'll wash your back."

He laughed and whispered something in spanish into her ear. The couple touched and kissed all over each other as they left the backyard. Tye stood up, dusting off his pants and feeling completely ignored but his feelings weren't hurt at all. He decided to instead go in the house to help his father and Avery with the campaign.

"Yo," Spence shouted from the yard next door, "Are you busy?"

"Not really," Tye said.

"Let's hangout before I head to work. We can play some video games or something."

Tye used to be into video games but had grown out of them. "Okay."

He made his way over to Spence who was sporting a boner in his black basketball shorts.

Tye chuckled as he walked with him into the house, "Why is your dick hard?"

"You broke it," Spence said, "It's been hard since you touched it."

"Jack off and it'll go away then," Tye said as he rolled his eyes at Spence's silliness.

They headed into the living room and Spence booted up the video game system. The entire time he let his erection swing freely, not bothering to readjust it in his pants. From every word he said to every move he made, it seemed as Spence was doing his best to come off as cool. Tye remember being that way around Isaiah in high school. That was his way of saying please fuck me without using any actual words.

Spence sat on the couch and passed Tye a controller. They started playing a racing game. At first Tye wasn't into it but started to have fun after a few races. Spence sat lounging back on the couch with his hard dick poking up in his shorts the entire time. Into the house Avery entered and Spence quickly sat up and hid his erection under a pillow. Avery paused for a moment as he stared at them.

Avery cleared his throat, "So, you guys playing the game, huh?"

"Yeah," Spence answered, "Just chilling before I go to work."

"Did you call your mom?" Avery asked.

Spence nodded and focused on the game.

Avery made his way around and forced himself in between them on the couch. There was an awkward silence as he just sat there watching the play the game. In his head Tye drifted off into some fantasy that involved him getting tag teamed by the father and son. He then could only wonder what thoughts they were having about him.

"Who's driving which car?" Avery asked as he rubbed at his narrow jaw.

"I'm the red one," Spence answered, "Tye is the blue one. What do you want?"

"I'm just watching," Avery said, "Tye, you're winning?"

"Yeah," Tye said as he kept his focus on the TV.

"You're really good with the turns Tye," Avery said.

"Dad, stop dick riding," Spence said.

"Hey, watch how you talk to me, we had this conversation," Avery said.

"No, we rarely talk. I'm not trying to be rude, just stating the obvious," Spence said.

"Well, it's hard to do when you're always on your computer," Avery said, "I regret buying it for you."

"It's funny because I've always felt like something you've regretted."

"We'll talk later," Avery said, "I'm going upstairs."

Before Avery could move, Spence paused the game and stood up, his erection gone, "Hey Tye, let me show you something in my room."

133

Spence walked off and Tye got up and followed after him, leaving Avery sitting on the couch with his face twisted up in frustration. They entered Spence's room that was once Avery's man cave. The bed of pillows was still in the center of the floor but not as neat as Avery used to keep them. Before Tye could ask what Spence wanted to show him, he turned around to find him standing butt naked. Already Spence's dick was hard again.

"What are you doing?" Tye whispered out, "Your dad might be listening at the door."

Spence turned on his radio, "There. Now, he can't hear us. I can't believe he was on that couch with us."

"It was awkward," Tye said.

"But anyways, you said you were going to suck my dick, remember?"

"I said maybe," Tye said.

"Can you please do it before I have to get to work? I have to be out in like...ten minutes. I'm mad that I wasted so much time playing the game, but I needed to work up the courage to ask you. Just when I was about to say something my dad's sickening ass walked in cock blocking. Please, Tye. Please."

Tye could not take his begging any longer, "You're so silly, man."

"Is that a yes?" Spence asked with a slick smirk.

Tye got down on his knees, "Only because you said please."

Tye licked his lips before slipping Spence's dick into his mouth. This wouldn't be the first time he sucked dick in this room. Spence breathed heavily and rubbed at his chest while staring up at the ceiling. Tye was loving his long dick more than he actually wanted to. The last dick he sucked was Brian's and it was nowhere as good as Spence's. Tye was caught off guard as Spence started to fill his mouth with nut.

Spence held Tye's head still as he kept on squirting, "Please stop moving. Please."

Tye swallowed down Spence's nut and started to laugh.

Spence pulled his dick out of Tye's mouth and started to get dressed quickly, "Why are you laughing?"

"You're so mannerable and shit," Tye said, "Please this, please that. It's cute."

"Shut up," Spence said as he laughed, "You liked it though?"

Tye stood up from his knees, "Oh yeah, good dick and good nut."

Spence face lit up at the compliment as he stepped into his sneakers and turned off the music. "I gotta go."

Spence rushed out of his bedroom and Tye walked out after him to find Avery in the kitchen putting up a glass.

"Bye," Avery shouted after his son only to receive no response. He looked to Tye, "What did he show you?"

"Huh?"

"In his room," Avery said, "He said he had something to show you."

"Some computer program I cared nothing about," Tye said, "Your boy is a geek."

"And a smart ass," Avery said, "I should've taken in one of my other kids. He's the only one who agreed to come. Spence is a good kid, but I brought him here to build a relationship. Instead, I can barely stand him and all he does is talk back to me. If he decides to leave I won't be upset at all. Just disappointed that we didn't bond."

"It'll work out."

"I know what can't work is you two being friends," Avery said, "He's an eighteen year old computer geek. I know you Tye, you two have nothing in common. Don't feel sorry for him, he'll find real friends eventually. What I'm saying is try to distance yourself from him more. I'm actually not even comfortable with you two being locked up in his room."

"You're jealous," Tye said as he stepped close to Avery, "I guess going straight hasn't been working."

"I'm not jealous."

"You think I'm messing around with your son?" Tye questioned.

"Are you?" Avery asked, nerves and panic in his eyes, "Tell me the truth."

"No. I just hang with him when I'm bored."

Avery pulled Tye close and shoved his tongue into his mouth. Less than a few minutes ago, the man's son's dick was in his mouth. This kiss was very wrong. Tye tried to pull back but Avery would not let him go. He had to get Avery off of him. Tye reached down and grabbed Avery's balls as tight as he could.

"Fuck," Avery said as he stopped kissing Tye.

Tye set his balls free, "Man, let's not go there again. We ended this."

Avery grabbed his crotch, "I regret it so much. That was a bad choice. I hate Shelia, I hate my son, and I hate not being able to fuck you. I'm only helping your father with his suicide campaign just to have a reason to see you all the time. When I fuck Shelia, you're on my mind. And I'll be honest. I still have photos of you on my laptop. Shit, I even have videos of you stripping for me and last night stole some of your underwear out of your bedroom while you were out." Avery pulled out his dick, "Only you can get me this hard."

Tye was not fooling around with both father and son. No matter how much it turned him on. He started to leave only for Avery to grab him, turn him around, and push him up against the kitchen wall. The man moaned and groaned as he aggressively dried hump Tye from behind. Tye just stood there, feeling sorry for Avery, letting the man hump him.

"I'm going to nut," Avery said as he pushed up against Tye harder.

Tye started to feel the lower part of his shirt getting damp, "Really?"

Avery pulled back panting heavily, "Fuck. What did I do?"

Tye touched at the nut stain on the back of his shirt as he faced Avery whose dick was dripping, "Hump me."

Avery put his dick away and looked away from Tye, "Forget everything I just said. We're done."

"Get it together man," Tye said.

He left the house with Avery's nut on the back of his shirt and the man's son's nut in his stomach.

22 - Posters

Tye remembered a short period in life when all he had was his hand. Chaz was gone, Avery was gone, and so was Perry. Things had started with Dom and ended horribly. And now things were back to the norm. Tye had a stable of men ready and willing to fuck him. Avery wanted him bad, Spence was in awe of him, Brian sent him cabin invites often, Isaiah was dangerously in lust with him, and Bam sent videos of himself booty clapping for his enjoyment. The only person who managed to behave was Chaz, the husband to be.

Tye got up and could hear the lawn mower running outside. He looked out of his window to spot a sweaty Spence mowing the backyard looking as if he was about to faint. Spence spotted Tye and instantly started to act all macho and unbothered by the early spring weather that actually felt like summer heat. It was easy deciding who would get his attention between the father and the son.

Avery had once again retreated back into his role of the good husband seconds after dry humping another Tye. While all Spence wanted was more and more of him. Tye decided to entertain Spence. He raised his blinds a bit revealing his nude body. Spence nearly crashed the lawnmower as he did a double take. Tye laughed and pretended he was performing oral sex on his fingers.

137

Spence just stared in awe as if he was witnessing the grand ending of a movie. Tye shook his dick from side to side and turned around and bounced his butt for Spence a bit. Spence wiped sweat from his brow as he bit his bottom lip. Tye waved at Spence and lowered his blinds. The father and son were more alike than they ever knew. Tye took a shower and headed downstairs to find his father, mother, Rodriguez, Avery, and Shelia gathered in the living room. Everybody was seated why Shelia stood front and center.

Shelia looked to Tye, "Are you a part of this or what?"

"He is," Jolie said, "He's my son. Herbert's son. He's a part of everything we do."

Shelia blew out a heavy sigh, "Then have a seat, Tye."

Tye sat down next to his mother and the woman kissed him on the cheek.

"Anyways," Shelia said, "The primaries are already down to three candidates including Herbert. Which means Herbert has a good chance of winning if we play things right. But the heat is about to get turned up on him. We need to be more focus. So I've taken some time off from the hospital to officially become Herbert's campaign manager."

"We don't need a manager," Jolie said, "This is a group effort."

"I'm sorry JoJo but it doesn't work that way," Shelia said, "This campaign needs a manager and that's me. Already some past clients of Herbert art out there spreading lies for Bernie. And we even have some flaws right under the roof of this home," Shelia said as she looked to Rodriguez, "But I'm going to keep this campaign running smoothly. I've set up a local interview for Herbert. He will tell the town his story and state his issues before Bernie drags his name through the mud. JoJo and Tye, expect to take part in that interview. All you have to do is sit down next to him, smile, and answer the tough questions."

"Wait," Tye said as he raised his hand, "You went from asking if I was a part of this to tossing me on TV."

"You were going to do the interview no matter how little you cared because you love your father," Shelia said.

"I do, but I don't feel like talking about my pictures on TV," Tye said.

"Then you should've never bent over and taken them," Shelia said, "Plain and simple. Answer for your sin."

"Ease up on my son," Jolie said, "And stop calling me JoJo. It's Jolie, SheShe."

"I won't ease up on your son because the press won't," Shelia said, "And they won't ease up on your escape to Mexico. I don't know the details but Rodriguez being here is a dumb idea, no disrespect. At least get him a hotel outside of town. People will eventually notice his block head walking around the house."

Rodriguez touched at his head of dark hair, "I have, block head?"

"Sir, don't make this about you," Shelia said as she held her palm out towards Rodriguez, "This is about Herbert. So, Tye stop whining about your pictures, Jolie hide your boy toy, and let's get focused. You three have to come out looking good after this interview. It could sink Herbert if it goes poorly. Are we all on the same page?"

Herbert stood up, "I am. And I'm ready to get back to work."

"I'm taking Spence out to hang campaign posters," Avery said, "Spend some time with him."

"And Roddy and I are going shopping," Jolie said, "I'll need a new dress for the interview."

"Make sure it's conservative," Shelia said, "Because so far you've been dressing like a stripper-hippie."

"And you dress like you're going clubbing with a bunch of twenty year olds," Jolie said, "I mean, I'm just saying since we're handing out fashion advice here. Anyways, I'm heading out. If I'm needed call me. And don't worry about Roddy. I'll tell whoever asks that he's my body guard."

After the back and forth between Jolie and Shelia, Tye found himself not in the mood to deal with people today. Instead he hung out upstairs in his room. He wondered what role he would play if his father actually beat Mayor Bernie. Tye was sure he would remain on the man's payroll. He still lacked the desire to go to college or to really start a career. Tye simply didn't feel like playing by society rules at the moment and officially starting an adult life. He was having too much fun, though being the walking town scandal was nothing to be proud of. Tye browsed around the web and ended up watching some porn. There was a knock on his room door and he hit pause on the video.

"Come in," Tye called out.

Into the room entered Chaz wearing fitted grey slacks and a light blue dress shirt.

Chaz shut the door, "Hey."

"What are you doing here?" Tye asked.

"Kendra is at her bachelorette party and the twins are out of town at some sort of medical expo. I stopped by to ask your dad if he needed help hanging posters or anything. And I was just wondering if you want to come with me. I really need somebody normal to talk too. Because Kendra has begun to live in this fantasy princess world, Bryant is in the dark about everything, and as you know, Brian is insane."

"How has he been treating you since you refused to fuck him?" Tye asked.

Chaz sat on the edge of the bed, "He doesn't invite me to the cabin anymore. And has been a constant force of negativity. I think he's trying to force me to apologize or something crazy. And I'm sure that would involve me having to fuck him which I refuse to do ever. I legit can't stand him. Hell, I even hate Bryant for simply looking just like him. When Kendra and I are married, I'm pushing hard to get far from her brothers."

Tye sat up and closed his laptop, "Well...I'm doing fine," He joked.

Chaz laughed as he rubbed at his square jaw, "How are you doing you brat?"

"I'm good."

"Have you gotten over that coma guy mess?"

"My dad keeps up with it mostly," Tye said, "There's not much we can do but wait for him to wake up."

"Who are you fucking outside of the cabin crew?"

"That was a quick change of subject."

Chaz shrugged, "I want to know."

"I've had only two dicks in me within the last couple of months, Brian and Bam's."

"Yeah, I've been fucking Bam. He has some good ass," Chaz said.

"I actually topped him at his place so I know exactly what you're talking about."

"I don't like him though," Bam said, "He's sneaky. Fucking for gain. I suggested he cater the wedding because he sort of insinuated that I owed him and we had to look out for each other. So, be careful fucking him. Because when his ass is out, so is his hand."

"I have nothing to give so he let me fuck him for nothing," Tye said, "But because of your warning I'm going to be a lot more careful around him. I like bottoming more anyways and I think I'm going to end up letting the kid next door fuck me. He's inexperienced as hell but I feel as if he doesn't have any ulterior motive."

"That kid next door is lucky then. We never had a good fuck."

"You came in me and my life and dipped out," Tye said.

Chaz nodded, "In another life I would fuck you right now."

"You're getting married now," Tye said, "All we can do today is hang up some damn posters."

Chaz stood from the bed and grabbed at his crotch, "Yeah, let's go do that then. This conversation is making me think dirty things about you."

Tye got up from his bed, open to the idea of sleeping with Chaz again but in another life of course.

23 - Live

Though it was Herbert's campaign, Shelia was acting as if it was hers. Tye didn't know how, but Shelia managed to convince him that this campaign was his priority. He didn't know if it was simply because she caught him at a time when his sex life was on pause, no longer heading to the cabin because of the lack of Chaz. Tye didn't really find much time to continue his fun with Spence and Bam was busy with work now that he had Isaiah back in town getting him catering jobs. But Tye did not mind Bam being occupied, based on what Chaz said the chef's booty was only a negotiating tool. Tye did not want to get roped into owing anybody any favors.

Tye was actually starting to believe his father could face off against Bernie without his reputation being ruined. So far Bernie had yet to come after his father unlike the other primary candidates. It was officially down to two now, Herbert and a business woman named Ava Knox who constantly mentioned her financial successes. Tonight Herbert would get to talk about his successes and plans for Riverbed to a popular local talk show host named Reva. And Tye and his mother was going to be there sitting at his side.

Tye and his mother was backstage in the greenroom while Herbert was in another area with Shelia prepping for the interview that would be live in twenty minutes. Jolie wore a red dress that hugged her body and neutral makeup. Shelia did all she could do to make Jolie look like an innocent housewife. She did

142

her best to also make the infamous Tye more presentable, but he refused to put on a suit. Instead Tye slipped on a purple polo shirt and some dark jeans.

Jolie paced back and forth in the greenroom, "I can't stand Shelia."

"Me either," Tye said, "Why does dad not see how much of a bitch she is?"

"Because they have always been really close as kids," Jolie said, "To be honest, I'm pretty sure they were destined to get married. But when they went to different colleges I swooped in. I know it's the main reason she can't stand me. We used to pretend to be close. She called me JoJo and I called her SheShe, but after you were born I became more focused on motherhood than that psycho. It's clear she still wants Herbert, right?"

"I guess," Tye said, "I still can't believe I was so blind about her feelings towards me."

"We women are really good at pretending to like somebody," Jolie said, "Don't let her bother you though."

"She doesn't," Tye said, "If I was a woman...I would smack her."

Jolie laughed, "You're not a woman though. You're a young man. One that I'm proud of."

"You're talking as if you're about to unpack and make yourself back at home."

"I don't need to be here to baby you," Jolie said, "You have to leave the nest."

"I get that," Tye said.

"And when are you going to do that?" Jolie asked.

"I love dad," Tye said, "I like being around him, working for him, that man makes leaving him hard."

"And that's why it tore me up for a bit," Jolie said, "But I grew out of the hold he had on me. It's still there though. I look at him and want to stay, but then I realize how incredibly boring he was. It was like being married to a brick wall. But a very kind brick wall. Just...promise me one day you will leave him and go start your own life."

"I will when I know I'm ready," Tye said.

Shelia barged into the greenroom, "It's time."

"Finally," Jolie said as she brushed at her dress, "I want to get back to Roddy."

Shelia rolled her eyes, "Focus on your husband tonight. He's been prepped thoroughly and is ready to take on this challenge. I

143

just hope that you two are equally as ready as him. Don't let Reva make you sweat. If she asks a difficult question, smile, nod, and answer it using common sense." She looked to Tye, "And be prepared to talk about your pictures and King."

"I know that, trust me," Tye said.

"Then I'm sure you're ready to answer to your ways," Shelia said, "Let's go."

Shelia led Jolie and Tye from the greenroom into a hallway. They followed her through the series of halls out to a cozy set. A mahogany round table was placed before a camera and a fireplace burned in the background. Herbert was already sitting at the table and the plump, dark-skinned, Reva was off to the side getting her braided hair sprayed with some product. A crew member motioned for Jolie and Tye to get on stage and sit at the chairs placed on each side of Herbert. The bright set lights shone down on them.

Herbert tugged at his suit jacket, "That light is hot as hell. Do you two feel that?"

"I'm sure it's been done on purpose," Jolie said, "People love seeing a politician sweat."

"I'm not a politician," Herbert said, "I'm trying to do a good thing."

"Dad, you have signs, campaign ads, and a scandalous marriage, you're a politician," Tye said.

Reva joined them at the table, "Herbert, you're a foolish man."

"It's nice to see you too, Reva," Herbert said.

"You guys know each other?" Tye asked.

"We've crossed paths at some events in the past," Herbert said.

"I'm good friends with Bernie," Reva said as she formed a sinister smirk, "We both researched Herbert last night."

Jolie rolled her eyes, "And yet Shelia thought this interview would be a great idea."

"Your husband had to face the town at some point," Reva said, "And I got the most eyes on my show."

Herbert let out a heavy sigh, "I'm not intimidated by whatever attack you and Bernie have come up with."

Reva brushed her braided hair back, "Let's see how big you are then. We're live when the lights dim."

Reva took a quick sip of water from a bottle on the floor and the lights went dim. An instrumental intro tuned played as Reva was handed a stack of papers. She set down the papers, faced the camera, and welcomed the viewers to her show. Reva started with Jolie and introduced each member of the family, ending with Herbert. Right out of the gate she came out swinging. She started asking Herbert questions about failed ventures like his book and clients he had to pass on to more experienced experts. She was doing her best to make Herbert look like a failure. But he didn't give up the fight. He focused on the issues and the people of Riverbed, all of them.

Reva looked to Jolie, "How's Mexico?"

"Fantastic," Jolie said, "I've helped plenty of people during my time in the Peace Corp."

"What kind of woman leaves her husband for months?" Reva asked.

"A woman who trust him," Jolie said, "I know he will remain faithful to me and the people of Riverbed." She looked off camera a bit toward Shelia, "He's my husband. And has always been my husband. No matter who else wants him, I know he will remain mine. This is the type of loyalty the people in Riverbed need."

Shelia tightened her face at Jolie.

Reva noticed the tension between them, "Your campaign manager doesn't seem to like that answer."

"She's a campaign manager," Jolie said as she faced Reva, "Nothing is never good enough for her."

"Whatever you say," Reva said. She turned her attention to Tye, "You took any pictures lately?"

Tye softly laughed, "Nope. You?"

"Yes, but not the type of pictures you like to take," Reva said, "Did you love King?"

"What?"

"Did you love King? Is that why you took those photos for him?" Reva asked.

"He was okay," Tye said, "Sorta crazy, but we all are."

"I'm not crazy," Reva said, "But you might be. Especially based on those pics you sent."

"I don't get how that makes me crazy. I'm sure Bernie has some pictures of you on his phone."

Reva snarled at Tye, "Bernie is a good man. My close friend."

Tye rolled his eyes, "In Riverbed that can mean anything. Next question?"

Reva turned her focus back to Herbert and things stayed that way for the remainder of the interview. Tye looked brave on the outside, but during that entire back and forth he was sweating bullets. He figured Bernie and Reva had dug up a lot more about his bedroom activities, but they had nothing. Still he stayed on guard until the interview was over. Afterwards, Reva gave Herbert a cold hug and didn't even bother addressing Jolie and Tye. They headed out to the car and Herbert drove while Jolie and Tye boasted about how they handled the interview.

Shelia looked in the backseat, "You two were rude."

"Reva was rude," Tye said, "And got put in her place."

"Exactly," Jolie said as she high fived Tye.

"Herbert came off professional," Shelia said, "While you two were ready to pick a fight and sling dirt."

"I didn't sling any dirt," Jolie said.

"You did," Shelia said, "At me. So let me say this, Herbert is my friend. Right Herb?"

"Since we were five," Herbert said as they turned into their neighborhood.

"So watch how you address me," Shelia said as she pointed her finger at Jolie.

"I can address you anyway I want too," Jolie said as she slapped Shelia's hand away.

"Do not, ever touch me, or try to insinuate that I want Herbert. I'm happily married," Shelia said.

"Trust me, you an Avery still look and always had looked awkward next to each other," Jolie said, "The only man you seem to be comfortable and happy around is Herbert. And I don't mind you having some ill feelings towards me. I've put up with that from you since the day we met and pretended to get along. But stop going after my son. It's childish and disrespectful to both me and Herbert. If you ever speak nasty to my son again I will snatch you up."

Shelia screamed as she crawled in the backseat and grabbed a handful of Jolie's hair. Herbert quickly pulled into the parking lot and blew the horn. While Herbert did his best to split them a part, Tye hopped out of the car and stood back watching two grown women tussle around in the car. Avery came rushing out of the house and Spence stood in the doorway watching the craziness. As Avery rushed into the car to try to pull the women a part, Tye joined Spence on the porch.

"What's happening?" Spence asked.

"World War III," Tye said.

"It looks like Shelia is winning too," Spence said.

Tye laughed, "I'm not even going to lie about that."

Herbert and Avery managed to drag both Shelia and Jolie out the car. Both of the women looked as if they had just got ran over by a stampede. They stood panting heavily and trying to break away from their husbands after finally getting years of pent up frustration out on each other.

"Stop this shit," Avery said, "Whatever is going on we're going to talk it out."

Herbert nodded as he held onto Jolie, "Exactly. I'll put on some coffee. We can talk all night."

"I don't want to talk," Shelia said, "I got a fight to finish."

"You're ghetto trash behind your medical degree," Jolie said, "Of course I always knew that."

"Jolie," Herbert said, "You don't mean none of that. Let's all calm down and go talk like civil adults."

Avery and Herbert did their best to drag the women inside. They all ended up heading over to Herbert's house to talk out the years' worth of issues. Not wanting to listen to that all night, Tye decided to hang out with Spence. Instead of sitting in the house, they sat on the back patio stairs of Avery and Shelia's home looking up at the stars.

"I saw the interview," Spence said, "You looked good on TV."

"Thanks."

"And the head was good too," Spence said.

Tye laughed, "Thanks again."

"I'm sorry Avery's weird ass was acting like that around you," Spence said.

"We talked about you right after you had left for work," Tye said, "He thinks I'm fucking you."

"Please I wish I was," Spence said, "But we can't do that, right?"

"Not on a crazy night like this," Tye said, "Horny ass."

"I can't help it," Spence said, "The world could be on fire and you'll be the only thing on my mind."

"And you're a poet, huh?"

"I try," Spence said, "I know we're not boyfriends or anything. But I like hanging with you."

"I would like hanging with anybody who sucks my dick also," Tye said.

"That's a big plus but you're also the only person in Riverbed I don't have to hide my past from," Spence said, "People act funny

147

when they learn I'm just some poor kid from Philly. I swear everybody in Riverbed seems to come from money and act like it too. Man, I was on the verge of going down to the hood and trying to find some people to hang with and then you took things with me to the next level. I got you now."

"You're a cool guy yourself," Tye said, "I guess you're one of the few friends I have."

"Are there other guys like us that you hang out with?" Spence asked.

"A couple," Tye said, "It's the main reason I kept hanging with your father. He was like me."

Spence scooted close to Tye, "I don't want to talk about him and you. That's nasty."

"I'm sure he would feel the same way about you and I."

"But I'm not an old man," Spence said, "He was."

"As long as the sex is good, I'm not complaining about how old a man is," Tye said.

Spence kissed Tye on the cheek.

Tye wiped at his face laughing, "Man, are we kids?"

"Your lips were turned away," Spence said, "I wanted to kiss you."

"Just ask for a real kiss next time," Tye said.

He faced Spence and pulled him in for a kiss. Though Spence wanted to kiss Tye, he barely could handle him. Tye was going to let his new friend see that he was far beyond pecks on the cheek. Tye reached down and could feel Spence's long dick about to tear through his pants. He rubbed on Spence's dick through his pants as he kept on making out with him.

Spence pulled back from Tye, "Can you suck my dick?"

Tye smirked, "Again?"

"Please," Spence said as he started to stand up.

Tye pulled him back down on the stairs, "Where are you going?"

"We can go in my room," Spence said.

"It feels good out here," Tye said as he unzipped Spence's pants, "We can do it right here."

Spence looked over his shoulder, "Outside?"

"Yeah," Tye said as he kissed him once again, "Chill back."

Spence leaned back on the stairs as Tye pulled his dick out of his pants. He smirked at a nervous looking Spence before going down on is dick. Tye didn't think he would find himself in this role so soon, the master training the student. This was like being with Perry all over again but with the roles reversed. Spence was new to the lifestyle and Tye was going to do his best to make it pleasurable but not traumatizing. He slobbed on Spence's dick, enjoying it in the back of his throat.

Spence kicked his feet and moaned as he watched Tye work his magic. Tye had zero concern about what was going on next door. He was only a bystander in the saga of Jolie versus Shelia. He was just glad somebody finally was able to go after Shelia. Tye simply tolerated her, Herbert was blind to her ways, and Avery was too busy trying to be a good husband. Tye was looking forward to how Shelia was going to treat him post-catfight.

Without warning, Spence started to full Tye's mouth with nut. Tye kept on sucking with a mouthful of nut as Spence moaned and groaned. The faces Spence was making were almost comical as Tye kept sucking his sensitive dick. Tye ended up bursting out laughing, spitting most of the nut from his mouth on Spence's pants.

Spence looked almost teary eyed as he sat panting, "What's so damn funny?"

"Your faces man," Tye said as he wiped his mouth clean, "Are you okay?"

Spence gently touched at his dick, "I'm good. Glad to have your ass as a friend."

Tye went down on Spence's dick one more time and came back up, "I'm going to go, okay?"

Spence just nodded as he remained lounging on the steps with his dick out under the starry sky.

24 - Over

Tye headed down into the kitchen to find his mother making a cup of coffee. Rodriguez was in the living room in just his boxers watching television. Tye had yet to get a recap of what had happened post the fight between his mother and Shelia. But based on the fact that Herbert was out campaigning with Shelia and Avery, things didn't work out in Jolie's favor.

Tye leaned against the kitchen counter, "Are you okay?"

"I'm fine," Jolie said as she sipped her cup of coffee, "I got my ass kicked for you, but I'm fine."

Tye softly laughed, "Yeah, Shelia did sort of have the upper hand from what I saw."

"I'll win in the end though," Jolie said, "I told Herbert that I'm done campaigning with him. As long as Shelia is running the show I'm keeping my distance. He begged me to come to this church breakfast they're all attending and I put my foot down. If my absence causes him the primaries, oh well. I can't be around Shelia anymore."

"And what if he wins without you at his side?" Tye asked.

"Then I played my hands wrong," Jolie said, "Cross your fingers for me."

"I am not," Tye said, "Because I now actually think he can win. Even after that interview with Reva he's still doing pretty good. But as you said, as long as Shelia is running the show there is no point in even getting involved with his campaign. I'm not going to be subjected to her abuse any longer."

Jolie started a second cup of coffee, "What are you doing today?"

"I don't know if you've noticed but I don't have a life."

Jolie laughed, "I see that. Kendra's wedding is right around the corner, you have a suit?"

"I don't do suits," Tye said, "But I'll throw something on."

"I met her fiancé," Jolie said, "He stopped by one day as Roddy and I were heading out."

"Chaz? Yeah, that's him," Tye said, "If you only knew the drama he's being put through."

"After getting my ass kicked I've had enough of drama," Jolie said, "I'm just going to drink my coffee and cuddle up with Roddy."

Jolie kissed Tye on the forehead and headed into the living room with Rodriguez. Tye headed back upstairs and found himself cleaning his room out of boredom. He found something to wear to the wedding and after watching some TV with his mother and Rodriguez took out the garbage. As he was dumping the trash he bumped into Spence who was coming home from work.

Spence approached him in the driveway, "Hey...friend."

"How was work?" Tye asked as he dapped Spence.

"It was slow so I left early," Spence said, "What are you doing?"

Tye shrugged, "It's a lazy day for me."

"I want to get in on that," Spence said, "Come be lazy with me. I can show you a program I coded."

"An actual program or do you just want a nut?" Tye asked with a smirk.

"It's a real program," Spence said, "But if I do end up feeling you up, you won't mind right?"

"It's what friends are for," Tye said as he playfully rolled his eyes.

He headed inside Avery and Shelia's house with Spence and into his room. They chilled out on the bed of pillows as Spence booted up a program he designed at work. He was doing his best to explain what the program actually did and Tye did his best to look captivated by the words coming out of Spence's mouth.

"To dumb it down, basically it goes through the registry wiping any errors and viruses out," Spence explained.

Tye nodded, "Oh."

Spence laughed, "Do I have to start over?"

"No, I get it," Tye lied, "So, the boy from Philly is also a computer genius?"

"I'm okay," Spence said, "Most of this stuff I learned in class or from the dudes I work with at the computer shop. But back in Philly I was always tinkering around with shit. If my laptop broke, my mom didn't have the money to get me a new one. So I would mess around with it until it started working again. Being resourceful has paid off."

"I had it different," Tye said, "If my laptop broke...my dad got me a new one that day."

Spence laughed, "Well, we all don't have it good like you Riverbed kids."

"But unlike most of us Riverbed kids you don't seem to be a manipulative shit head. Be glad you're not from here."

"You're not manipulative," Spence said.

"I have my moments," Tye said, "It's the reason my pictures ended up online. I lured a vulnerable person into my bed. And I'm reminded of that every day by the way some people look at me and whisper behind my back. In a way, all the judging has made me more aware of my shit head ways. I try my best to behave. Yet I do things like this."

"Like what?"

"You," Tye said, "You're the son of a man who once wanted to start a life with me."

"But I want this," Spence said, "You're not manipulating me."

"I know," Tye said, "But I should know better. Some people I should not sleep with. Because of me, a guy is in a coma and I can't even claim a bit of responsibility. Doing so would sink my reputation even more. I don't care about that, but I do care about how it would affect my father's life."

"Man, stop beating yourself up," Spence said, "It's not like you're out there fondling kids. It takes two to tango. And if guys like my dad and that dude in the coma want to sleep with you then they got to be ready to suffer the consequences. I do think about what would happen if we get caught together. And then I realize...I don't care. Shelia will blow up like expected and my dad would probably use it as a reason to get me out of Riverbed."

"You think he wants you gone?"

"I can feel it when I walk into the room," Spence said, "But I don't care. I just don't connect with him."

"Yet you two have so much in common," Tye said.

Spence shrugged as he closed and put away his laptop, "I'm fine though. As for you, just like I said, don't take all the responsibility when these guys you mess up end up screwing up their lives. You always seem to make it out unscratched though. You're the master of fucking around in Riverbed."

Tye softly laughed, "Thanks...I guess."

Spence kissed Tye, "No, problem."

"I guess we're done looking at your program?"

Spence stuck his hands under Tye's shirt, "I just wanted to get you in my room."

Spence and Tye wasted little time getting naked on the bed of pillows. Tye grabbed Spence's dick that was harder than he had ever felt it before. It was clear Spence was way excited about this moment, most likely expecting more than a handjob or some oral pleasure. Tye finally decided to stop teasing Spence and give him the full treatment. He mounted Spence who looked confused and nervous. Tye smiled down at him and slowly started to slide down on his dick.

"Oh fuck, are we going to do this?" Spence asked as his voice shook.

Tye managed to get halfway down on Spence's dick, "We've already started."

Spence started to moan so loud that Tye had to cover his mouth just in case somebody came home. Tye kept riding Spence's stiff dick while doing his best to keep him quiet. As expected, Spence started to nut only after a few minutes of being inside of Tye. His dick remained as hard as it was when they had first started fucking and Tye wasn't complaining. Spence's nut provided the much needed lube as Tye enjoyed bouncing on his dick. Tye did most of the work, Spence no more than a sex toy right now. He was Tye's live action dildo.

"I'm done, Avery," Shelia's voice sounded throughout the house.

"What do you mean done?" Avery shouted.

Spence and Tye quickly got up from the bed of pillows and got dressed. Spence led his way out of his room and they watched from the doorway as Shelia and Avery bickered back and forth in the living room. Tye was trying to wait for the right moment to slip out of the backdoor to simply avoid the wrath of Shelia.

Shelia pointed her hand in Avery's face, "Men. You are horrible creatures."

"I don't understand what you're talking about honey."

"After the breakfast Herbert had the nerve to ask me to leave the campaign because he needs Jolie at his side," Shelia explained, "After that bitch left him and I stuck by his side, he had the nerve to ask me that. It was insulting. I'm an educated woman. And I no longer can deal with all the stupidity of the men in my life. If Herbert needs Jolie more than me, he can have her. He'll learn his lesson once again and I won't be there to console him."

"You're overreacting," Avery said, "Relax."

Shelia motioned at herself, "Relax? Me? No, you relax."

"What?"

"I'm having a moment, Avery. A moment of freedom. And I can't be completely free as long as I stay around tolerating your lies. I know what you are. I've seen your browsing history. I see the way you stare at guys around town. But, I put on a good act just to make things seem normal. But there's nothing normal about being married to a gay man."

Avery gulped, "I...I'm not gay."

Shelia smacked him across the face, "Don't insult me. I'm done with you, Herbert, and Riverbed."

"Hold up," Avery said, "You're really talking some crazy shit."

Shelia glanced back to notice Tye and Spence watching her and Avery's marriage crumble.

Shelia snarled at Tye, "You could've been my son. I should've gotten with Herbert and give birth to his child, not Jolie. I would've raised you so much better. Instead, Jolie put a mess on Herbert's hand. A nude photo taking, freeloading, disrespectful mess. It makes me sick seeing you and your mother, the downfall of my friend." Shelia let out a heavy sigh to calm herself, "But you know what. I'm moving on. Avery, you can have this house of lies, because I'm going to the Bahamas and I'm going to find the sexiest man on that Island and finally get some real dick."

Shelia looked Avery up and down, scoffed, and stormed out of the house.

25 - The Wedding

As one marriage crumbled, another was being officially bonded. After a beautiful ceremony that involved a lot of tears from Kendra, Tye found himself at the wedding reception of Chaz and his new wife. The wedding ceremony was just another Riverbed event for most. It was a chance for them to show off their cars, clothes, and jewelry. And most importantly, this was everybody's' chance to go all out and when it came to the wedding gifts.

While Tye got the couple a simple gift card, others got them everything from puppies to ski trips. Chef Bam catered the wedding dinner and his food was delicious as always. Bam was walking around letting those dining know which dishes would appear in his new cookbook he was still in the process of prepping. Tye was enjoying a fish dish as Bam took a seat next to him.

"Hey stranger," Bam said as he sat down next to Tye.

"I'm a stranger to you now?"

"You don't respond to my text or come to the cabin anymore," Bam pointed out.

"I've been busy playing politics with my father," Tye said.

"I heard he's about to win the primaries," Bam said, "I'm available for catering. I would love to cater a victory dinner."

Tye had to give Chaz his props, Bam's hand was always out indeed, "And I would love to attend one."

Bam stood up from the table, "Don't be shy, call me sometime."

Tye flashed Bam a phony smile as he walked away to continue promoting his cookbook. After finishing up his food, Tye made his way around the reception room chit chatting with the familiar faces of Riverbed. He looked across the room to find his mother looking happier than ever on his father's arm. Tye was sure it was because she officially trumped Shelia who had been gone from Riverbed for weeks now.

Avery was not in attendance of the ceremony or life period. The man spent a lot of time home alone, Herbert the only person who was able to communicate with him. Tye always figured Avery would be happy about Shelia leaving him. But Tye didn't worry himself about how the man's complex mind worked. He had his own problems, like an approaching Isaiah.

Isaiah shook Tye's hand, "It's nice to see you."

"Out of all the people here you just had to come talk to me, huh?"

"I love the sound of your voice," Isaiah said, "I can't help it."

"When are you getting married?" Tye asked, changing the subject.

"Married?"

"Yeah, it's rare the head preacher in town is single. Are you dating?"

Isaiah smirked at Tye, "Cute."

"I'm serious," Tye said, "Are you going to marry some blind sheep of a woman who'll believe you're straight?"

"I can always sit a wig on your pretty head."

"Can you not be creepy for one moment and have a real conversation with me?" Tye asked.

"Fine, we can do it over dinner," Isaiah said with a smirk.

"I'm walking away now," Tye said as he turned away from Isaiah and bumped into the groom.

Chaz stood looking a bit tipsy, "Hi Tye."

"Are you okay?" Tye asked.

"It's my wedding day," Chaz said, "The happiest day of my fucked up life."

"Has Brian attitude towards you changed at all?" Tye asked.

"He asked me to fuck him again last night. I was in the shower and he slipped in with me only to get kicked right out," Chaz said, "Crazy, right?"

"Well, you're officially married to his sister now. I'm sure he was just trying to get at you before you said 'I do'."

"As I stood up at the altar looking at Kendra, I realized she looks a little bit like her brothers," Chaz said, "I had to hold down my vomit as I said my vows to her. Shit, I didn't even write my own vows. I found it on the internet and changed the words around a bit. Brian is in my head and I can't get him out. And you know what, Kendra has suggested we live in the cabin. And Bryant likes that idea while Brian doesn't for obvious reasons."

"You can't live in that cabin," Tye said, "That'll be beyond fucked up."

"I know that," Chaz said, "Can you talk her out of it?"

"Me? Kendra and I are friends but I don't think I can change her mind about where she wants to start and raise a family. I'm sorry Chaz, but you're going to have to fight her on this cabin nonsense. I don't think you're going to have a very happy marriage if you don't."

"I should just scream my truth," Chaz said, "Starting with the moment I started fucking you and exposing the cabin crew."

"Yo," Tye said, "Don't do that."

"It'll get me away from Brian, my marriage, everything that makes me unhappy."

"It'll fuck up so much," Tye said, "I'm not in the mood to live through another scandal."

Chaz shrugged, "Fuck it then. I'll just have to suffer. Thanks for not caring."

Chaz walked off and headed to the bar. Tye felt horrible for Chaz and wished he could help him out of this situation. But he had to think about himself, his father's campaign. Chaz simply needed to find the courage tell Kendra his naked truth, minus the details of the other men involved. For the rest of the night Tye was treated to the disaster of Chaz trying to keep it together. Herbert was busy chatting up Isaiah, working hard for his endorsement. Kendra and her friends were on the dance floor for most of the night and she even convinced Tye to dance with her once. The music stopped as Brian grabbed a microphone.

"I need everybody's attention for a moment," Brian said.

"Everybody listen up," Bryant voiced.

Brian motioned at Bryant, "My brother and I are so proud right now. We are proud that our little sister has found her perfect man. As kids, we always had to protect her. We didn't grow up in the most desirable or safest part of Riverbed. So protecting our sister was something we spent a lot of time doing."

"Especially from boys," Bryant added, "Almost every knuckle head liked her and we would have to get involved. Eventually she left Riverbed and met Chaz. And when we were invited to come down to Virginia and meet, my brother and I had our fingers crossed the entire time. The moment I met Chaz I knew he was the right man for our sister."

"And I had the same reaction," Brian said as he looked to Chaz and smirked.

Chaz did his best to form a smile and hide his disgust of Brian as Kendra grabbed his hand.

"Anyways," Brian said, "We put together a little slide show of the happy couple. Enjoy."

Bryant hit play on the laptop and photos of Chaz and Kendra started to shuffle on the wall of the reception room. The crowd chuckled and awed at the pictures of the couple displaying their love for each other. But all the chuckling stop when the slide show was interrupted by a video. In the video an oiled up Chaz was penetrating a man in a leather mask from behind. All that could be heard throughout the reception hall was the man in the mask groaning out Chaz's name as he was being taken from behind.

Bryant rushed up to the laptop and quickly slammed it closed. All eyes in the room shifted towards Chaz, including Brian's who wore a subtle smirk. Chaz stood as still as a statue, his eyes locked on the wall where the video had played. Tye lived through this before. He knew how it felt to be exposed. And didn't ever want to feel what Chaz was experiencing right now ever again. Kendra let loose of Chaz's hand and stepped away from him. She smacked him in the back of the head twice and stormed off crying. Her bridesmaids and mother chased after her.

Bryant ran up to Chaz and punched him to the floor, "You sick fucker!"

Chaz lay flat back on the floor staring up at the ceiling. Bryant went in for another punch only for Herbert to pull him away. Herbert struggled as he tried to hold a cussing Bryant back. A couple of other men jumped in and helped Herbert dragged Bryant out of the reception hall. Isaiah stood shaking his head in shame at Chaz and whispering with a woman who stood near him. Tye debated whether he should go help Chaz up. Before he could decide, Chaz stood up on his own and slowly made his way out of the reception hall.

"Everybody," Brian said, "Thank you for being here. But it's clear this night did not end so well."

The guests started to leave the reception hall as the room filled with chatter and some started to text. A new scandal had hit Riverbed and soon the entire town will know. Tye didn't even have to guess who was responsible for exposing Chaz. He made his way over to Brian. Before he could get a word out, Brian raised his hand to Tye's face.

"Don't even bother defending him," Brian said, "He deserved what he got."

"Nobody deserves that," Tye said.

"I told him from the start to play by my rules," Brian said, "And he didn't."

"You ruined his life, embarrassed your sister, over some dick."

"It wasn't about dick," Brian said, "Chaz and I had an agreement. And he stopped honoring it."

"No matter how you try to spin it, this was about some dick," Tye said, "You're fucking petty as hell."

"Chaz brought this upon himself," Brian said, "End of story. And based on the way you're talking to me, I wish I had you on video because I would gladly expose you all over again. Get off your fucking high horse Tye. You were in that cabin like everybody else fucking your little life out. You weren't thinking about Kendra or how it would hurt if the truth came to light."

"And neither were you and you're her fucking brother," Tye said, "Her blood."

Brian thought about it, "Well, I guess in the way exposing Chaz was a good deed."

"Tell that to your heartbroken sister," Tye said.

Tye stormed away from Brian. He did not expect this night to end like this at all. Tye wasn't going to convince himself he wasn't just as guilty as Chaz, Brian, and all of the others in Riverbed who secrets could cause so much damage. But watching Brian destroy his sister's marriage and Chaz's life without little care made it clear that he was not as bad as him. Tye arrived outside to find his mother watching as Herbert did his best to calm Bryant down.

Jolie looked to Tye, "That poor girl, right?"

"It's horrible."

"And you felt bad for him at some point?" Jolie asked.

"Mom, not now," Tye said, not wanting to admit that he felt really bad for Chaz.

"Be honest with the ones you love, son," Jolie said, "Your dad knew about Roddy. I did not like the idea of sneaking around with another man even though Herbert and I were not officially together anymore. I let him know during a very long conversation that though I was his wife that another man had my heart. I'm sure Kendra would not be as broken down if Chaz had been honest with her. He's a coward."

"Mom, coming out is not an easy thing to do for a lot of guys like me and Chaz."

"I get that, but he didn't have to marry the damn girl," Jolie said.

"You're right about that," Tye said.

Tye wondered if he was just as guilty as Brian now. He knew before even sleeping with Chaz that he was marrying Kendra, yet he still pursued him. For himself and father, Tye had pushed for Chaz to continue living a lie. Brian on the other hand dragged that lie kicking and screaming into the light. Tye didn't know how he came to this conclusion, but maybe Brian's actions were in a way a good thing after all for his sister.

26 - Cali

Tye didn't know how it was possible, but somehow the Chaz incident was all Herbert's fault according to Mayor Bernie. Photos were on the local news of Chaz hanging up campaign posters for Herbert. Once again Herbert was connected to somebody whose private sex life was exposed to Riverbed. Herbert was now spending most of his time defending the values of those Bernie claimed he was close with.

Tye was too busy feeling bad about what happened to Kendra to even pitch in with the campaign. He knew it wasn't directly his fault, but at the same time he was a horrible friend to her. There was a knock on the house door and he got up to answer it. On the porch stood Chaz looking a bit rough, his eyes red and clothes wrinkled.

"What happened to you?" Tye asked as he stepped aside.

"I spent the last week in a hotel drinking and crying," Chaz said as he entered the house, "Is your dad here?"

"Nope, what's up?" Tye said as he shut the door.

"I wanted to apologize to him," Chaz said, "I see how they're attacking him on the news about me. They even reported that I was his assistant. All I did was hang up some fucking posters. I feel like the biggest piece of shit right now. I destroyed Kendra and now your father's campaign."

"My father will recover," Tye said, hopeful.

Chaz sat down in the living room, "I won't."

Tye joined him on the couch, "Not really. People still look at me funny."

"How do you live like this?"

Tye shrugged, "You realize that eventually another scandal will change the subject."

"Well, I'm already for somebody else to fuck up," Chaz said, "I'm a shitty person."

"We both are and so are a lot more people in Riverbed," Tye said, "But when it comes to Kendra we both wronged her. Hell, I even wronged you. For a split second you wanted to scream out your truth and I pushed for you to keep your mouth shut. I was fine with you never telling her. And that was fucked up of me."

"You were protecting yourself and your dad," Chaz said, "In my head I called you selfish but then understood."

"It was selfish of me, but thanks for understanding where I was coming from. Have you talked to Kendra?"

Chaz nodded, "Yeah. She cried for an hour and forgave me."

"Did you tell her about Brian?"

Chaz shook his head, "Nah, I'm not as sick as him. I'm not going to go around exposing people. But while Brian is probably taking it as a victory, Kendra and Bryant sees it as a major embarrassment. Kendra has already moved back to Virginia. And I heard that instead of opening up a practice here, Bryant wants to relocate to Georgia. He doesn't want to be known as the doctor whose sister got screwed over by a monster. And apparently Brian is going with him. They feel it's what's best for their family name or some bullshit like that."

"And I guess you'll be leaving next, huh?"

Chaz shook his head, "My tuition at the med school is paid in full. If Kendra and I had ended up moving, my father would've covered the cost for me to attend a new med school and for our home. But my parents are just as upset with me as Kendra. I'm not abandoning med school, instead I'm just going to stick around Riverbed and deal with the whispers and stares. You seem to be doing alright dealing with these assholes around here."

Tye nodded, "Yeah. And just wait until all the men start trying to sleep with you."

Chaz stood up, "I'm definitely not going to let that happen. I need to focus on med school. That's my priority."

"Smart move," Tye said, though he was sure Chaz would crack.

"Anyways, let your dad know I was here."

Chaz left and Tye got up and locked the door. He turned away only to hear knocking coming from the back door. He made his way through the house to the back door and opened to find Spence standing carrying a duffle bag in one hand and wearing a backpack.

"I hate to say this," Spence said, "But I got to go."

"Go?"

"I can't stay in that house anymore," Spence said, "Avery has lost his fucking mind ever since Shelia left him. So, I'm taking his credit card, buying me a plane ticket, and going to stay with my cousin in Cali. I'm glad you were home though. I had to come and say goodbye. You were the only person in this town I enjoyed being around."

"Yeah, you were cool too," Tye said.

"I'm really going to miss hanging out with you."

"I'll miss you and all your geekiness also," Tye said with a smirk, "But trust me, you're going to make a lot of guys happy."

Spence kissed Tye, "Bye, Tye."

Tye smirked at him, "Be good in Cali."

Spence rushed off and left for California. Tye had no contact with Avery since Shelia left him. Herbert busy with his campaign and with Spence now gone, Tye figured he should go check up on the man to make sure he hadn't done anything crazy to himself. And in a way Tye was curious to know why Avery was so down and out about a woman he didn't want leaving him. He walked next door and entered Avery's house through the back door. Tye headed upstairs and knocked on Avery's room door.

"Who is it?" Avery said.

"Me, Tye."

"I'm not home," Avery said.

Tye pushed into the room anyways to find Avery lying in bed beneath the covers, "Yes you are."

"Leave me alone," Avery said.

"I'm just here to let you know that Spence is gone," Tye said.

Avery shrugged, "I don't care."

"And that your credit card paid for his flight."

"Good," Avery said, "I regret bringing him to Riverbed. It only showed me that I'm a shit father."

"I'm sure you tried," Tye said. He sat down on the bed, "What's wrong with you?"

"Shelia," Avery said, "That bitch told my bandmates everything. I'm out of the group."

"Why?"

"Because they're bitches," Avery said, "Afraid of traveling with a gay man. Because that's what I am. There's no hiding from it. She told the people who matter most to me the lie I kept away from them. How could she be such a bitch? I've officially lost everything because of that woman. Music was my life."

"You can still do music," Tye said, "Start your own group, write songs, or manage new talent."

"I shouldn't have to start over," Avery said, "I'm an RnB legend."

"You should be glad to start over," Tye said, "Free from Shelia."

"I'm too old to be restarting life," Avery said.

"No you're not. You get to do everything different now, as yourself."

"Like what?"

Tye wanted to help Avery. He needed to do some good after wronging Kendra so greatly, "Fuck me."

"What?" Avery said as he raised his brows.

"You can fuck me without having to worry about Shelia coming home," Tye said, "Shit, you can fuck anybody."

"I still have to start over," Avery said.

Tye pulled back the sheets revealing Avery's nude, scrawny body. Between Avery's legs sat his flaccid dick.

Tye grabbed Avery's dick, "But you get to fuck me while you rebuild."

Avery remained silent as Tye massaged his dick. Inch by inch the man's dick grew in Tye's hand. Once he was hard, Tye went down and stuck Avery's dick in his mouth. He missed the man's dick. Tye didn't even know how he convinced himself that Spence could deliver better than his father. Avery sat up and helped Tye strip out of his clothes. Once nude, Tye and Avery started to make out.

"Why are you doing this with me?" Avery asked.

"You need it," Tye said.

"So, we're not done?"

"Do you want us to be done once again?" Tye asked.

"I dreamed so much about fucking you," Avery said, "I miss your hole around my dick."

Tye softly laughed, "I won't lie. You got some good dick."

Avery lay back and jerked his dick, "You want it?"

Tye mounted Avery, "Deep."

Tye slowly sat down on Avery's dick. It felt so good having the man deep inside of him once again. Slowly, Tye started to ride Avery. The man was free. No wife to hurt. Tye still knew them being together was a stretch. But this wasn't love, but instead a lust Tye was glad to be able to experience once again. He rubbed at Avery's hairy chest as he rode his dick hard. Tye could tell by the smirk on Avery's face that this was exactly what the man needed to be delivered out of his depressing state. They made out as Tye grinded on Avery's dick.

"You're right," Avery said as he grabbed at Tye's waist, "I can rebuild."

"There you go," Tye said, "Rebuild. Takeover."

"I'm already thinking of new tracks," Avery said.

"If you get a Grammy, you better thank me then."

Avery laughed, "I will."

"You gonna bust in me?" Tye asked as he hugged his hole tight around Avery's dick.

Avery sat up a bit and tightened his face as he started to pour nut into Tye, "Fuck."

Tye kept riding as Avery continuously filled his hole with nut. It felt as if the man hadn't nutted in months. So much nut spilled from Tye's hole as he kept riding Avery's dick. Tye pulled up off of Avery's dick and looked back to find his booty splattered with nut and the man's dick drenched. Avery kissed Tye on the lips as he fingered Tye's wet hole.

27 - Blind

All of Tye's free time was now spent with Avery. If he needed a break from the campaign, he went over to Avery's. If he got bored, he went over to Avery's. Things between them were strictly still lust, but Tye was loving how better Avery's stroke game had gotten. It was as if being free from Shelia had awakened a better man in Avery. Avery had even started working on new songs and trying to put together a solo tour. Instead of spending this morning with Avery deep in him, Tye and his mother was helping his father with a speech. He had one more big speech to give before Riverbed voted for who would face off against Bernie.

"It needs more spice," Jolie said from the couch.

Herbert paced back and forth in the living room before them, "You think?"

"She's right," Tye said, "You sound too nice. Toss in some scare tactics."

"Fine," Herbert said. He stopped and faced him, "Can you believe we've come this far?"

"You did all the hard stuff," Tye said.

"Yeah, I just stood and looked pretty," Jolie added, "You're the one who got yourself this far."

"Still, having you two support me meant so much," Herbert said, "And though it's clear she's not the most popular person in this house, Shelia was a big help also. I did manage to get in touch with her even though the conversation was short. In time, she will forgive me. We've had many of fights throughout our friendship and always come back together."

"Mhm, sure," Jolie dismissively said, "Back to your speech."

Tye's phone vibrated and it was a text from Bam. Apperently he finished the first draft of his cookbook and wasn't going to move any further with it without the second opinion of somebody who would be brutally honest with him. He was inviting Tye over, basically begging for him to come critique his cookbook. Already hearing his father's speech various times and sure the man would deliver in the end, he decided to answer 'yes' to Bam's constant begging.

Tye stood up, "I have to head out for a min. I'll be back."

"Where are you going?" Jolie asked.

"Chef Bam wants me to look at the final draft of his cookbook," Tye said.

Herbert snapped his fingers and pointed at Tye, "Ask if he can cater my election night party."

"I will," Tye said as he left.

He made his way over to Bam's condo. Bam answered wearing some jeans only.

"I'm surprised you said 'yes'," Bam said, "It's as if you've been avoiding me."

"I've been busy with the campaign like I said before," Tye said, "By the way my dad wants you to cater the election night party."

"I can't do that," Bam said, "Because if he loses I don't want to ruin my reputation with whoever beats him. Tell him to call me after he wins."

"Ouch," Tye said, "Business comes first, huh?"

"I'm sure he's a nice man, but yeah, business comes first," Bam said, "Anyways, do you want to see the book?"

"Yeah," Tye said as he sat down on the couch.

Bam went into his room and returned with a thick book of loose papers, "Here it is. My future."

Tye grabbed the draft of the book and started flipping through the pages, "Shit, I'm already hungry."

"That's a good thing," Bam said, "All original recipes. Nothing like I've done before."

"It would be better if I could taste everything," Tye said as he kept flipping.

"And the book will be bundled with coupons so they could buy some of the exact products I used to craft the original recipes," Bam said, "I've already reached out to a lot of the food brands that'll supply specialty coupons. There's still a lot of tweaking to be done and the task of finding a publisher. But I'm sixty percent done with the book."

Tye closed the book, "All things seem to be going good for you then."

"Yup," Bam said, "We should celebrate."

"How so?"

"Well, ever since you abandon the cabin crew we haven't fucked at all," Bam said, "I've discovered some kinky shit since we've last been together and would love to try it out with you. So, how about we go to my room and I show you exactly what I'm talking about?"

"Why not do this with Isaiah?" Tye asked.

"Because you fucked me better," Bam said.

Tye remembered what Chaz told him. Bam slept with most for gain. "Why are you into me?"

"Because you fuck me best," Bam said, "Now let's go."

Bam yanked Tye up from the couch and dragged him to his bedroom. On Bam's bed were two blindfolds.

Bam stripped out of his jeans, climbed on the bed, and put on one of the blind folds, "It's simple. You put on the other and we explore each other bodies using our hands." Bam bend over in the center of his bed and made his booty clap, "But you can start by feeling around inside of me. Just promise to where the blindfold."

Tye instantly remembered how good fucking Bam felt. He stripped down, slipped on the other blind fold, and did his best to navigate his dick inside of Bam. Bam let out a moan and clapped his booty cheeks faster as Tye slipped deep in him. Tye wore a smile the entire time as he slid into Bam. He liked this entire blindfold situation. It made Bam's moans and touch more pleasing. He fucked Bam blindfolded until he was on the verge of nutting. Tye pulled out and they ended up feeling around blindly until their lips met. Bam and Tye rolled around on the bed kissing.

"Lay on your stomach," Bam said, "I want to lick your hole."

Tye smirked and got in the position. He arched his booty. The anticipation of waiting to feel Bam's tongue against his hole made this moment much more sensual. Tye felt a vibration through his body the moment he felt Bam's wet tongue against his hole. He started to moan as Bam pleasured him with his tongue.

"Oh fuck," Tye said, "Shit."

"Feels good, huh?" Bam asked, "Wait until you see how this dick feels."

Tye pulled his cheeks apart as he felt Bam's dick head poke at his hole. Bam arched his back more as Bam started to dig him out. Tye didn't know if it was the blindfold or not, but Bam was really delivering some good dick, better than he ever did. Tye moaned as Bam's thighs slapped against his.

He could feel his hole splitting open each time Bam dug in balls deep. Tye just kept moaning his name out loud, not wanting the chef to stop. He dug his face into the mattress which caused his blindfold to shift upward a bit. Before he could pull his blindfold back down Tye notice Bam was standing bed side jerking off. He quickly sat up and yanked off the blindfold to find Isaiah fucking him.

Tye quickly jumped from the bed, "What the fuck?"

Isaiah sat in the center of the bed with his dick twitching, "Tye, relax."

"Are you fucking kidding me?" Tye shouted, "You niggas are sick!"

"Tye," Isaiah said as he reached out trying to calm him.

Tye slapped Isaiah hands away, "Don't ever fucking touch me."

"You're overreacting," Bam said, "You were enjoying his dick. He's a good fuck."

"Say something again, Bam and I'll knock your teeth out," Tye said, "Why?"

"I can explain," Isaiah said, "You know how I feel about you. And you refused to give me a chance to prove it. So, I asked Bam to help prove how much I want you. He agreed to help me win you over in exchange for some catering jobs. Don't be mad at him. This was all my doing. You were loving everything I was doing to you. And we can do so much more together if you just accept me. Please."

"This is rape," Tye said, "I should fucking call the cops."

"Rape?" Bam said as he laughed, "Please."

"I didn't do this to hurt you," Isaiah said, "I was desperate to prove my love to you. We were making love."

Tye started to get dressed, "Don't you ever speak to me again, Isaiah. And I mean it this time. Fuck you."

"No fuck you," Isaiah snapped, "I've been nothing but nice to you. But if you want to keep being nasty to me, I can play the same game. So, if you don't get back in this bed and finish what we have started I won't endorse your father. I will make sure every person in Riverbed vote against him. Walking out of this room right now will literally end his campaign. A campaign he can win easily with me and the church on his side. It's your call."

"For somebody who loves me that's a fucked up thing to do," Tye said.

"I played clean and now I'm getting dirty," Isaiah said, "Tye, get back in this bed."

"I'm going to leave you two to work things out," Bam said as he left the room.

Tye stared Isaiah in his eyes, "I used to be obsessed with you."

"I know that," Isaiah said.

"And then I realized you were fucked up like the rest," Tye said.

"Only because I had to survive," Isaiah said, "Do right for my family, their legacy."

"Fine, do the right thing and leave my father's campaign alone."

"No, you do the right thing and save it," Isaiah said, "Because I will destroy it."

"My father is a good man, with a good message," Tye said, "He'll win without you."

Tye stepped into his sneakers and left the room. As he made his way from Bam's condo he debated turning around. But he refused to sleep with Isaiah. Tye put all his hope into his father's message delivering the man a victory. He supported his father and would do anything to make sure the man would win, but he could not sleep with Isaiah.

28 - New Job

This was what defeat looked like. After so much hard work and long nights, Herbert lost the primaries after Isaiah and his parents made a surprise at his opponent's campaign event. Isaiah even spoke, telling voters that Herbert was a good man but not what Riverbed needed right now. Herbert was speechless, no clear idea why Isaiah endorsed his opponent. But Tye knew. He was the reason his father sat at his kitchen table in silence. Jolie joined Tye in the living room as Rodriguez was out packing their bags into the taxi.

Jolie sat down next to Tye, "Are you okay?"

"Not really," Tye said, "Look at his face. He's hurt."

"There was nothing we could do," Jolie said.

Tye knew that wasn't true. "Still, it sucks seeing him that way."

"Herb and I talked last night," Jolie said, "About our marriage. We're going to officially get a divorce."

"Are you going to marry Rodriguez?" Tye asked.

Jolie shrugged, "I'm not thinking that far ahead yet. Anyways, I have a plane to catch."

Tye hugged his mother, "Don't stay gone so long this time."

"Or you can come see me in Mexico," Jolie said with a smirk, "And bring Herbert."

"I'm pretty sure he can use a vacation," Tye said.

Jolie kissed him on the forehead, said goodbye to Herbert, and left her family once again for Mexico. Herbert remained in his somber state as Tye got up and went to go stand outback. He could not sit around watching his father mope around all day, the guilt too much. Over in his yard Avery was cutting his grass.

Avery stopped and waved to Tye, "Is your dad still in the dumps?"

"Yeah," Tye said, "You should take him out?"

"I can't today," Avery said, "I have a meeting with a label to sell them some new songs I wrote."

"That's good," Tye said, "I see starting over is going good for you."

"I have you to thank," Avery said as he winked at Tye.

Tye smirked and the man got back to mowing his back lawn. After sitting outside for a bit, Herbert rushed outside.

"Tye," Herbert exclaimed.

Tye was thrown off by the man's sudden mood change, "What is it?"

"I got an email," Herbert said, "An email that has just made my week a lot damn better."

"Really?" Tye said, glad for some good news.

Herbert sat down on the stairs with Tye, "The College upstate saw my interview on Reva's show. They've been following me and were disappointed that I didn't make it out of the primaries but at the same time they're glad because they want to offer me a job. They want me to oversee and new department at the college. A department that focuses on helping those from low income areas get GEDs and enroll into the college soon after. I'm beyond thankful for the opportunity."

"Upstate? Does that mean we're moving?"

Herbert shrugged, "Let's see how this all plays out before we get to that part. Though Riverbed is full of idiots, I like some of them for some reason. I like my house, the few friends I have, and being close to the place I grew up from. I'm going to do my best to work at the college and do my sessions here. It'll be a nice distraction from my defeat and officially losing my wife."

"And I'll be here to help you, dad," Tye said.

"And hopefully find your way also," Herbert said, "I know you will."

Herbert patted Tye on the back and headed back inside. Tye didn't know what he was destined to do or exactly what he

172

wanted to do in life. He did know that he had a knack for making men do crazy things or even betray the ones they were supposed to love for him. But there was one man in Tye's life who he knew spending time with would not likely lead to any drama. He got up and made his way over to Avery's house. He let himself in through the backdoor to find the man sweaty from cutting grass sitting at his kitchen table drinking a bottle water.

"What's going on?" Avery asked, "Was that your father I heard out there talking?"

"Yeah," Tye said, "He got a job offer. And that seemed to bring him out of his funk."

Avery got up from the table, "That's good. What are you up too?"

"Forever searching for my purpose in life," Tye said.

"Maybe you were put here to make people happy," Avery said, "Shit, you make me happy."

"I'm sure I do."

"Especially when you're butt ass naked," Avery said as he pushed up on Tye.

Tye laughed, "Ew, you're all sweaty."

"Let me get out of these clothes then," Avery said as he stripped naked, "Better?"

"No," Tye said as he grabbed Avery's hard dick, "But it's turning me on anyways."

"You gonna get naked for me?"

"It's what I do best," Tye said as he took off his clothes.

Avery pressed his naked body up against Tye's and they started to makeout.

29 - House of Sin

Tye was having a party and the guest list was pretty short. Avery was one of the names on that guest list along with an artist he was now managing named Zach. Along with those two, the third and final name on that very short list was Chaz. Tye found himself upstairs in his bedroom that he had been sharing with Chaz for the last couple of months getting dressed. Facing a body mirror, Tye slipped on a dark t-shirt and some blue jeans that he had rolled up above his ankles.

Chaz stood next to him in the mirror tugging at the white dress shirt he wore and khaki shorts that hugged his tone thighs. They both playfully bumped into each other as they got dressed before sharing a kiss. Tonight they would be celebrating Chaz's medical school journey that was now heading towards a residency at a hospital just outside of Riverbed. The politics of the elite town had made it impossible for Chaz to land a residency within the city limits.

But even though people stared and whispered, Tye was glad Chaz did not give up. And the moment he came close, Herbert was kind enough to offer him a bedroom in his home. The man cared little about what his friends and neighbors would think, Herbert working upstate at the university and now only a part-time resident of Riverbed.

Tye was glad to see everybody he cared about moving on with their lives and not letting the distractions of Riverbed get in their paths. He now at the age of twenty-five was in away finally discovering his purpose. Tye was following in the footsteps of his father, helping those who weren't born into the world of nice homes, extravagant parties, and luxury cars.

Chaz checked his reflection once more, "How do I look?"

"Fuckable," Tye said.

Chaz chuckled, "You too."

There was a knock on the house door.

"They're here," Tye said, "I'll get the door."

"And I'll start setting the table," Chaz said.

They both shared another kiss before heading downstairs to let in their guests. Tye liked the place where he and Chaz found themselves when it came to their friendship. Since the moment Herbert took Chaz in Tye was there to support him. They had long talks sometimes until sunrise, laughed about some of the horrible things said about them, and some nights found themselves sharing a bed together. Not much had change from that point. Tye knew he liked Chaz. But wasn't going to struggle trying to label what they had. They were happy being around each other and that's all that mattered.

Tye opened the front door to find a tall Avery who wore black slacks, a red dress shirt, and a dark blazer.

"Damn," Tye said, "You got all dressed up just to walk next-door, huh?"

"It's a habit," Avery said, "If I'm going to a party in Riverbed there's no such thing as being overdressed."

"They have us trained like monkeys," Tye said as he laughed. He looked to Zach, "What's up, man?"

Zach, who was about half of Avery's age, had a small frame but carried a big voice. Many mornings Chaz and Tye were woken up by Zach who had a bad habit of sitting out in the backyard writing songs and singing to himself. Zach was dark-skinned, had a welcoming smile, and big eyes that always made him look as if he was about to scream out in excitement. He wore some torn dark jeans and a white polo shirt that fit his lean body.

"I hope you can cook," Zach poked as he dapped Tye.

"Hell no," Tye said, "I ordered everything from a restaurant."

Avery slipped into the house, "You know what. This doesn't feel like the house of sin."

Tye rolled his eyes at the title that most of the town had branded the residence. For some reason both him and Chaz being under the same roof bothered a lot of people in town. And they mostly weren't shy about how they felt. Plenty were still upset about what Chaz had done to Kendra and looked down on those who associated with him.

"It must be on fire in here then since the wife beater has stepped through the door," Tye quipped.

"I still have to find out the source of that rumor," Avery said, "I never touched Shelia."

"In many ways," Tye joked.

Avery caught the joke before he burst out laughing, "Yep, you're demonic."

Once Zach was inside Tye shut the house door and they all went into the kitchen. Chaz had plated all the sushi they had ordered and opened two bottles of white wine. He greeted their guest with daps before they all sat down and started to eat. Most of the dinner conversation focused on the reason they were all here tonight, Chaz's medical journey.

But they eventually did get on the unavoidable topic of Zach and Avery's plans for his artist. He had met Zach at a late night visit to a gay bar, a place Avery visited frequently once his sexual relationship with Tye had dried up. Zach's cute face, voice, and allegedly impressive head game, was enough to convince Avery to dedicate all his time to working behind the scenes to make him a star.

"When's the album coming out, Zach?" Chaz asked.

"There is no album yet," Avery answered for him, "Right now I want to focus on getting his name out there the old school way. Next week we're going to start traveling all over the country doing open mic nights. I'm going to be renting out my house to help cover a lot of the traveling charges. He's going to be performing some original songs I wrote. I'm excited for this trip. We're going to be spending a lot of time together and forming a healthy manager and artist relationship."

Tye could only imagine Avery's long dick in Zach, "Hey, I forgot to tell you I'm volunteering down at the bookstore warehouse."

"You're actually going to work?" Avery teased.

"Yeah, but only on the weekends. And instead of getting paid they'll give me free books that I can take down to the community

176

center," Tye said, "The last bunch of books I took down there went to good use. Most of the kids were reading them instead of coloring in them or trying to use the pages to role blunts this time."

Avery laughed, "I swear you and your father are so patient."

"I'm not as good as my dad when it comes to working with the inner-city youth," Tye said, "He's my inspiration though."

"Yeah, I talked to him earlier. He's loving his job at the college. His last GED class produced the most graduates since he had started the program there," Avery said, "He talked about that and mostly wanted to know if you were taking care of his home though." Avery surveyed the home, "I'll tell him you're doing a good job. The value hasn't been driven down one bit."

"But yours has gone up," Chaz butted in, "Is the hottub working yet?"

"It is actually," Avery said, "I'm thinking maybe we all should finish off these wine bottles in there."

"I'm in," Zach said, "The steam is good for my vocal chords."

Chaz stood up, "I just want to relax and get drunk as hell. Because I know once my residency starts I'll have little time to do so."

Tye used his hands to play a beat against the table, "I guess it's hottub time then."

They did a rush job of clearing off the kitchen table before taking the backyard over to Avery's yard. It didn't take Avery long to warmup the hottub he had purchased during his phase when he realized Shelia was no longer around to manage his spending. They all stripped down to their underwear and climbed into the hottub with their drinks. Like most gathered tonight in Riverbed with drinks in their hands, they found themselves gossiping about the many rumors floating around town.

"I heard Isaiah will finally be taking over his father's role," Avery said, "He'll be head preacher soon."

Tye scoffed, "They deserve him. He's psychotic."

"I think you meant to say a rapist," Chaz said, "Because that's basically what he did to you. And Bam isn't quite so innocent himself."

"A psychotic rapist then," Tye corrected.

"Hold up," Zach said, "You got raped by a preacher? Man, they're so many crazy stories in this town."

177

"It wasn't violent," Tye said, "He and a friend of his pulled a bed swap on me while I was blind folded. There's nothing fun about pulling off a blindfold and finding the wrong dick inside of you. Especially the dick of a man who plays mister innocent but has spent a lot of time tearing down people like Chaz and I for mistakes we made in our lives. I don't think running down the streets screaming the truth about somebody as powerful as him will gain any traction though. Nobody will believe the town whore got raped by a child of the almighty."

"No, I'm the town whore now," Chaz said as he motioned at himself.

"And for some reason they all think I beat my wife," Avery added in, "But I've heard worse rumors."

Zach looked a bit shocked, "My hometown is nothing like this. We're chilled down in North Carolina."

"Speaking of Isaiah, his lil friend Chef Bam's book is doing great on the best sellers list," Avery said, "He was able to get out of Riverbed but not escape the drama. His parents are now trying to sue the hell out of him, claiming he never paid them for their managing duties. I heard it's a move out of desperation because his father is filing for bankruptcy. And speaking of bankruptcy-"

"-Enough," Chaz said laughing, "Can we not talk about other people's lives for a moment?"

"Fine," Avery said, "Let's talk about yours. What are your intentions with my best friend's son?"

"To support him," Chaz answered, "He stood with me when nobody would."

Avery nodded, "Tye does that."

"Because I know how it is to have that Riverbed spotlight of shame on me," Tye said.

Zach stood up and started to dance, "I love the spotlight."

Zach's underwear were so damp that you could see everything he was packing below. Avery reached out and squeezed Zach's booty as he kept dancing around to a beat in his head. It was clear the alcohol was starting to kick in. Zach plopped down on Avery's lap and started to kiss at the man's face.

"Okay, now this party is getting good," Tye said.

Chaz reached over and grabbed Tye's hard dick beneath the water, "Yup, you're in party mode."

Zach looked over to them smirking, "Are you two entertained?"

Chaz and Tye nodded.

Avery raised his hand, "I am also."

Zach slipped off his underwear and shoved them into Avery's mouth, "Good."

Zach stood back up revealing his dark chocolate booty and dick to them. He danced around a bit more before putting his hand between his legs. Zach bit down on his bottom lip and started to finger himself in front of everybody. Avery kept watching with Zach's underwear in his mouth. Zach started to moan as he kept fingering himself.

"I love his moaning voice better than his singing voice," Chaz said.

Tye decided to make Chaz's night even better. He slipped off his own underwear and joined Zach in the middle of the hottub. Tye sucked Zach's dick for a bit before standing up and making out with him. They both made out for Avery and Chaz in the center of the hottub while rubbing at each other's bodies and letting their hard dicks sword fight. Tye started to finger Zach's tight hole while the singer did the same to his mocha toned bubble butt. They both kept using plenty of tongue while kissing each other.

Avery looked over to Chaz, "Is your dick about to pop?"

"Man you have no idea," Chaz said, "This is beautiful."

"I know. What man can deny this sexy ass sight?"

"A straight man," Chaz quipped, "But I'm so happy not to be straight because of moments like this."

"Be lucky you've accepted it while you're young," Avery said, "I spent so many years trying to hide it and then sneaking around. A lot of nights I sit up hating myself but self-forgiveness is a thing. I'm much happier now overall though. Especially because I get to help Zach's career blossom." Avery reached out and pinched Zach's booty, "And of course fuck him. He's tight as hell."

"Really?" Chaz said, "Tye is a good fuck too."

Avery laughed, "Trust me, I know. I taught him everything he knows."

"Fucking liar," Tye butted in before he went back to making out with Zach.

Avery laughed, "I guess we'll agree to disagree."

Chaz reached out and grabbed at both Zach and Tye's booties, "We found two good guys then."

"Hey Zach," Avery said, "Are you cool with Chaz?"

Zach looked to Chaz, "Yeah." Zach focused back on making out with Tye.

Avery motioned to Zach's booty, "Chaz, treat yourself."

"You sure?" Chaz asked.

"Hey, I've had your guy...now it's your turn have mine."

Chaz nodded as he stood from the water revealing his toned, dark, body. He slipped off his briefs revealing his black dick that looked strong and thick enough to break a cinderblock. Chaz positioned himself behind Zach and slowly slipped his dick into him. Tye and Zach resumed making out as the singer was being fucked. Chaz took slow strokes into a softly moaning Zach.

"Tight, right?" Avery asked.

"Oh yeah," Chaz said, "You met the right dude at the club that night."

"I know," Avery said, "He's talented in many ways."

Chaz pulled his dick out of Zach and sat back down in the water, "I'm impressed."

Tye and Zach stopped making out and sat on the laps of their men. After watching Zach get dicked down Tye was ready to get some himself. He slipped Chaz's dick into his hole and started to ride him in the hottub. Avery sat on the edge of the hottub, took off his briefs, and Zach started to give him some head.

Tye always found it a bit challenging when it came to deep throating Avery's dick, but Zach was making it look easy. Tye kept riding Chaz's dick nice and slow as he watched Zach enjoy Avery's. After getting enough head, Avery bent Zach over the edge of the hottub and started to fuck him. It wasn't long before Tye found himself bent over beside Zach getting fucked by Chaz.

Tye and Zach found themselves making out again as their holes were pounded from behind. Out of the side of his eye Tye did catch Avery and Chaz share a dap and he could only smirk. The people in this hottub were in away the only friends he had. And Tye was not ashamed to share his naked truth and body around them.

Their fun moved outside of the hottub onto the wooden patio area that surrounded it. Avery and Chaz were turning tonight into a competition. They were both pulling out their stroke game and sex positions. Tye and Zach played along, simply glad to have two nice dicks deep in them. As they both rode the dicks of Avery and Chaz, Tye and Zach made a bet.

"I bet I can get Chaz to bust before Avery," Tye said.

"It's on," Zach said.

Avery and Chaz got up and stood side by side. On their knees, Zach and Tye were trying to suck their way to victory. Zach used his hand to jerk Avery's dick as he kept on sucking it. Tye had grown very familiar with how Chaz's dick liked to be pleasured over the last year and focused all his attention on pleasing the head.

But Tye found himself in trouble when Avery started to bust in Zach's mouth. Zach revealed a mouthful of nut to Tye as proof before swallowing it down. Tye came in a close second when Chaz busted in his mouth and he also swallowed. The night was still young. More wine was drunk as they lounged on the deck rubbing at each other's bodies, laughing, and naked.

30 - Home

Tye's night with Chaz, Zach, and Avery would never be forgotten. But he could not linger on that forever. It was time to get back to reality. Chaz's residency was starting soon and Avery and Zach had officially left Riverbed for a tour across the nation, going from one open mic night to another. Tye sat up in bed trying to shake off his sleep before heading to work at the book warehouse.

Next to him Chaz slept with a medical text book opened across his chest and sporting some morning wood. Tye thought back to all the men he had been with in his life. Of course he liked the majority of them, but since day one Chaz had kept his interest. Tye knew if they decided to discuss a label for them it would be boyfriends. That didn't' scare him at all.

He reached out and rubbed at Chaz's dick only for him to groan, swipe his textbook to the floor, and turn onto his stomach. As Tye slipped out of bed his cellphone started to ring and it was his father calling. He walked the upstairs hallway of the home as he chatted with his father.

"How's my house?" Herbert asked.

"It's good," Tye said.

"Is Chaz still staying there?"

"Yeah," Tye said.

"He's a good guy," Herbert said, "I like him."

"Yeah, me too. How's everything at the college?"

182

"I love it," Herbert said, "I'm respected here. The GED program has been a hit. I feel so free here, empowered. But I foolishly sometime miss Riverbed and my house. I can't wait to come home during the winter break and just sit on my couch. Hell, I might throw a party and invite everybody so I can rub in how great I've been doing."

Tye softly laughed, "That's very Riverbed of you, dad."

"Old habits die hard," Herbert said, "I want to come home to a clean house though."

"How about you just install some cameras so you can monitor me?"

"Fine, I'll ease up off of you. You're working today, right?"

"Yeah."

"I'm proud to see you following in my footsteps. I love telling people I've raised a son who cares about people."

Tye smirked, "And I'm proud to be the son of a man who cares even more."

"I'm going to go," Herbert said, "I've joined a speed walking club with some of the other professor's."

"Bye, dad," Tye said, "And don't break a hip."

"I won't," Herbert said as he laughed, "Love you."

"I love you too," Tye said.

Tye ended the call glad his father was free from the political games of Riverbed. He didn't think the man would be able to recover from attempting to unseat Mayor Bernie, but Herbert was still standing strong. Tye went to shower and slipped on some khaki slacks and a white t-shirt. Chaz was still sound asleep. He didn't bother him and instead ate a quick bowl of cereal and headed to work.

Tye drove to the book warehouse that was located on the border that separated the upper-class of Riverbed from the lower-class as some referred to them as. The book warehouse sold used DVDs, books, CDs, and plenty other items at discounted prices. The staff was a mixture of volunteers, paid employees, and those like Tye who worked in order to receive free merchandise for donation purposes.

He arrived to the book warehouse, clocked in, and focused on organizing some books. Four eight hours he would put books in alphabetical order, point lost old women toward the registers, and stop children from playing catch with the merchandise. As he worked Tye accidentally bumped into and old woman.

"Sorry ma'am," He said.

"Yes you are," The withered, mocha toned, woman snapped, "I know who you are. You live in that house of sin."

Tye let out a sigh. He was sure the woman was a member of Preacher Ramsey's congregation. They were all usually the most vocal when it came to criticizing him and the others around Riverbed who were shamed on a daily basis. This behavior wasn't promoted by Preacher Ramsey himself, but instead by his wife, the mother of a nagging Isaiah, Glenda.

Tye was beyond being polite to those like this woman, "Listen, lady-"

"-lady," She interrupted, insulted, "That is Miss Diane to you. Don't be disrespectful."

"Well Miss Diane please keep moving."

"You need help," Miss Diane screeched, "You're sick. And that other one living with you in the house is just as sick. He broke that poor girl's heart fooling around with men. He could've given her some kind of sickness. All you have to do is pray, both of y'all. Isaiah is supposed to be taking over the church soon. I hope having a good young man like him leading us will help bring lost boys like you into his church."

Tye wanted to tell her all he knew about the true Isaiah, "Are you done, lady?"

Ms. Diane smacked Tye in the face, "I said don't be rude."

Tye touched at his face embarrassed as he noticed others watching them. He rarely let people like Miss Diane get to him but she had no right to put her hand on him. Tye had a really long rant built up that he was ready to scream into the woman's face. But before he could get a word out Isaiah popped up and grabbed him by the arm.

"Ms. Diane, let me chat with him," Isaiah quickly said.

Ms. Diane's face lit up as she spotted Isaiah, "Oh hey, Isaiah." Her joy faded as she looked back to a fuming Tye, "This one lives in that house of sin."

"I know," Isaiah said as he yanked at Tye's arm, "Finish your shopping and I'll see you Sunday."

Ms. Diane raised her nose to Tye before walking off. Isaiah, who wore soft yellow slacks, brown dress shoes, and a light blue dress shirt, dragged Tye by the arm toward the back shelf of books. In his mind Tye was still planning on going after Ms. Diane. He pushed aside his anger with the woman as he realized

Isaiah had his hands on him. Tye yanked his arm away from Isaiah as they arrived to a secluded area of bookshelves.

"Don't fucking touch me," Tye said, "You got people like her putting their hands on me."

"I've never bad mouthed you," Isaiah said.

"Don't fucking lie to me."

"Fine, I did," Isaiah said, "But you know how it is. Relax."

"I just got smacked in a store full of people."

"My father has already spoken to Ms. Diane about her hands. She also has a bad habit of trying to beat other people's kids," Isaiah said with a smirk. He dropped his smile as he realized Tye found zero humor in this situation, "Listen, I'm sorry that had to happen. But what do you expect? You're living in that house with Chaz. Chaz is stained. And once you add in your past it only makes the situation worse. I'll be taking over my father's spot soon. I'll invite you into my church, help you win back the people of Riverbed but you can't do that with Chaz in your life."

"I'm not doing anything to impress you people. I've done it all before only to make things better for my dad. But just like I don't care what you hypocrites think, he doesn't either anymore."

"Dang it, Tye," Isaiah said, frustrated, "What happened to that guy who used to like me in high school? Why can't I have him back?" Chaz looked around before unzipping and pulling his hard dick out of his pants, "Forget him and be with me. Look how hard you make me. I think about you too much. My love for you is something I can't pray away. It felt nice when I was in you."

Tye couldn't believe how desperate Isaiah looked. He shoved Isaiah backward sending him bumping up against a bookshelf.

"Stay away from me," Tye said, "Don't ever fucking touch me."

Tye stormed off and went to the employee breakroom to gather himself for a moment and hope that Isaiah had already left the store. He could hear some of his co-workers whispering about him and snickering. Tye didn't say anything to them. The management team didn't tolerate much drama around the store and was quick to release troublemakers. He held his tongue before getting back to work.

The job seemed a lot more complex now. Tye's mind was stuck on the encounters he had with Ms. Diana and Isaiah today, he couldn't focus. Tye left exactly the moment it was time to clock out, not focused enough to pick out some free books to collect for his shift today. He arrived home to find a shirtless Chaz coming

185

downstairs. Tye met him at the bottom of the stairs, embraced him, and held him tight.

"Are you okay?" Chaz asked as he rubbed at Tye's back.

"They got to me today," Tye said.

"The bad ass kids?"

"No, Isaiah and some old hag named Diana. I'm so mad I let them get to me."

"What can I do to make you feel better?" Chaz asked.

"If you can't kill them, just keep holding me right now."

Chaz laughed, "I'll hold you then."

Tye buried his face into Chaz's toned chest and let out a growl of anger, "Fuck them."

Chaz kept holding him tight, "Just focus on all the good in your life."

"I'm trying to do that real hard right now. I don't know why I'm still in Riverbed."

"Don't let them win," Chaz said, "This is your home."

Tye looked to Chaz, "But we all have to move on sometime, right?"

"You're not trying to move on in this case. This is you running away because you're hurt. There's a difference," Chaz said, "You're the guy who encouraged me to hold my ground against these people. You can't go breaking down because of some old lady and a creep. Okay?"

Tye nodded. He stepped back from Chaz as his phone started to ring. It was an unknown number and Tye sent it to voicemail. Immediately a call came through again. Tye tried to recognize the number and once again sent it to voicemail. But the caller was persistent. Tye answered the phone.

"Who is this?" Tye asked.

"My name is Frank Sutters. Is this Tye?"

"Yeah."

Frank cleared his throat, "I work with your father at the college."

"Is everything okay?"

Frank stalled to answer.

"Hello," Tye said into the phone.

"I'm just calling to pass on some news," Frank said, "Early this morning there was an accident. Your father and several others were struck by a drunk driver while speed walking. There's no easy way to say this but unfortunately your father isn't one of the survivors," Frank started to weep, "He passed away, Tye."

"I have to go Frank," Tye said before he ended the call.

Chaz crossed his arms, "Who's Frank? A bill collector?"

"He's friends with my father," Tye said as he replayed the phone conversation in his mind.

Tye went over it word by word, trying to figure out where Frank misspoke. He repeated the process, but no matter how many times Tye kept trying, he could not change the man's words around, they kept coming out the same in his head. He hugged his arms back around Chaz.

"Tye, what is going on with you today? What's wrong?" Chaz questioned.

Tye pressed his ear against Chaz's chest, listening to his heartbeat, "My father's dead."

"Shit," Chaz said.

Chaz wrapped his arms tight around Tye and held him tight.

31 - Herbert

Tye had guests over. But it wasn't for a party. The majority of those who had attended Herbert's funeral were now crammed into the man's house mourning his memory. Tye wanted to spend his time upstairs in his room crying his heart out but his mother was doing enough of that at the moment. He found himself in the downstairs bathroom as the woman continued to weep as she leaned against the sink counter. She kept pulling tissue in and out of the upper half of the fitted black dress she was squeezed in.

"I'm a widow," Jolie cried, "I know we're not officially married anymore but I'm claiming it, dammit."

"I'm not arguing against that."

"I'm alone now," Jolie said.

To Tye it seemed as if his mom was really regretting leaving them behind, "You still have, Rodriguez."

"Oh that ended a while ago," Jolie said, "He left me for some bar whore. I talked to Herbert about it. Because of him I got through that heartbreak. But now that I realize it, I took Herbert's advice and really never got the chance to thank him. I'm horrible."

"You being here today is your thank you," Tye said.

"Do you want a chance to cry?" Jolie asked.

"I have," Tye said, "And I will some more. But for now, let's get back out there with everybody else. If dad was here he would want us out there talking to everybody and making them smile, not hiding away from them in the bathroom."

188

Jolie adjusted her dress, "I know, I know. Hey, did you see Shelia at the funeral?"

"No, I didn't notice her."

"We actually chatted for a short moment without fighting."

"Dad would also like that. Is she okay?"

"She lives in Vermont or something and is dating some unfortunate fool from the private practice she's managing now," Jolie said, "I really sort of zoned out of the conversation once she started going on and on about everything else. The more I heard her voice the more I actually wanted to have a rematch with her. But...for Herbert...and as the classy widow I am, I behaved."

"Good," Tye said, "Anyways, let's get back out there."

Tye and Jolie left the bathroom and entered into the crowded home. So many familiar faces were in attendance. A now pregnant Kendra showed up with her new husband that she had met in Atlanta. She was actually chatting with Chaz and smiling with him. Tye hoped others seeing Kendra be friendly with Chaz would take some of the heat off of him with the locals. But Tye knew the people in Riverbed rarely let others forget their past mistakes.

A woman wearing a black dress and giant matching hat approached Tye, "I was looking for you."

Tye did not recognize the woman, "Me?"

"I'm Dominique's Aunt Greta," The woman introduced, "I drove all the way here from South Carolina just to pay my respects. Your father has been calling almost every day to check up on Dominque's status and has been sending money when he could to help out. I wish I had the pleasure of meeting him in person before this had happen."

Tye hugged the woman, "Thank you for coming. How's Dom?"

"Not much has changed," Greta said, "But I know one day he'll wake up."

"Yeah. It's a horrible situation."

"I know we'll overcome it," Greta said, "I'll let you know the moment he wakes up."

"I'll be waiting for that day," Tye said.

"Excuse us," Brian voiced throughout the crowded home.

"Just for a moment," His twin Bryant added, "We just need to make a small announcement."

Tye was surprised Chaz and the twins were able to be under the same roof together. But tonight was indeed not about bringing up past feuds, but instead all about Herbert.

Bryant continued, "In our speech at the funeral we forgot to mention that we will be renaming our private practice down in Atlanta."

"Instead, it'll be named after the man who got us to this point," Brian said, "My brother and I have agreed to call our private practice the Herbert Medical Center."

There was a soft applause throughout the home. Brian and Bryant returned to chatting with the other guests in attendance. For the rest of the night Tye found himself waiting for everybody to leave. He heard plenty of stories about his father. Each was getting him closer to the moment when he just wanted to breakdown and cry.

Tye chatted with Avery who had returned alone from his tour with Zach momentarily for the funeral service. Avery only had more stories about Herbert that caused himself to shed tears. Tye needed a moment to collect himself so stepped outside on the front porch.

His eyes met with Isaiah who was making his way up the porch stairs in a black suit. Isaiah had also attended the funeral service and burial earlier, but kept his distance from Tye. Tye was sure Isaiah only took that precaution to save face, Riverbed politics always in motion.

"Leave," Tye said.

"Wait," Isaiah said, "I just wanted to come check on you."

"I'm fine," Tye lied.

"No you're not," Isaiah said, "You lost your father."

"I did. Now leave."

"Wait," Isaiah said sternly, "I came to check on you and warn you."

"Warn me about what?"

"Moves are being made against you," Isaiah said, "And once I find out more I'll let you know."

"I don't want to play any Riverbed games right now."

"That's too bad," Isaiah said, "Because everybody else is. And you're a target."

Tye wasn't going to ever let those against him in Riverbed win, "Bye, Isaiah."

Isaiah shook his head and let out a sigh before walking back to his car and leaving. Tye took a moment and dried away tears that were starting to make their way out of his eyes before heading back into the house. The evening went along and around ten

190

everybody started to leave. Tye and Jolie stood by the door hugging and thanking each person who showed up, even Brian. After all the guests were gone, Jolie headed up to the bed she once shared with Herbert. Tye and Chaz straightened up the house a bit before crawling into bed with each other.

"I was so nervous when I saw, Kendra," Chaz said, "But she was happy."

"I saw," Tye said as he lay staring up at the ceiling, "Did Brian say anything to you?"

"He's too much of a coward to do that. Bryant kept his distance also."

"I didn't get a chance to say anything to either of them, just a hug and a 'thank you' on their way out."

"I wonder if they were upset about you letting me live here," Chaz said.

"I honestly don't care because you're staying. You're all I have."

"Your mother is just down the hall."

"You know what I mean," Tye said.

Chaz nodded, "I do."

"You're all I have because my father is gone," Tye uttered out as he started to cry.

Chaz looked over to Tye, "I won't leave you, okay?"

"Okay," Tye said as he kept crying.

Chaz cuddled up with Tye. Tye cried late into the night. No matter how tired he was of shedding tears, Tye could not stop. The only thing making this night easy to get through was that he had Chaz cuddled up next to him. And Chaz did not move one bit or shut his eyes on Tye. Chaz remained being there for Tye as he mourned late into the AM.

32 - Win

Life in Riverbed went on for everybody except for Herbert.
Chaz had officially started his residency which meant he spent
less time home. Tye received all the support he needed from the
med student but with Chaz being around less he had to rely on
himself sometime to get through the tough moments. Those were
the days he could not get his father off his mind.

Today wasn't one of those days though the man could never be
forgotten. Tye had just returned from dropping two boxes of
books off at the youth center and was relaxing on the couch.
There was a knock on the front door. Tye got up and answered it
to be greeted by Isaiah who was holding some papers in his hand.
His first reaction was to slam the door on Isaiah's face.

"Wait," Isaiah said as he forced his way into the home, "I can't
just leave this time."

"Aren't you busy? You're being crowned king of the religious
crowd in Riverbed this Sunday."

It was the talk of the town. Preacher Ramsey was stepping
down and this upcoming Sunday Isaiah would deliver his first
sermon as head preacher.

"That's Sunday," Isaiah said, "You have a big problem that you
need to deal with now."

"My life is fine. I'm not getting involved in anything."

"Stop saying you're fine," Isaiah said as he raised the papers in his hand to Tye's face, "You're homeless."

"No, I'm not."

"Listen," Isaiah said as he hit his hand against the documents he held, "My mother is a very influential woman in this town. And you know she and I both have friends in high places. Through the bank where your father made mortgage payments an oversight was discovered. Yes, he owns this house but because of an error that came up for debate. An error related to him running a business out of his home and not paying all the necessary fees. Through the church the home was purchased via an auction."

Tye laughed in disbelief, "That doesn't make any sense. Plus, they can't auction off the house without informing me."

"You're acting as if people play fair in this town," Isaiah said, "This was all my mother's doing. There's a lot of people on her list of targets that she loathes. And you and Chaz are on that list. The church owns the house of sin and my mother plans on evicting you soon and renting it out. But all of this can be prevented. I hold all the power at the church which means I can hand this house over to whoever I want. And I'm willing to go against my mother to please you. All you have to do is give me a chance and I'll give you back this home."

"I'm getting a lawyer," Tye said.

"And you'll have to fight this from a motel," Isaiah said, "This is what happens when you try to turn your back on the games here in Riverbed. I warned you moves were being made. Together we could've worked to find out which move but instead you told me to leave. And now you've lost your father's home. And you can have it back this moment if you give me a chance to prove how much I love you. No lawyer can undo this. You'll find one to try but it'll be a long drawn out process that'll end with you homeless and defeated. I can fix this today."

Tye knew the right move would be to simply go find a lawyer. But why do that when he could fix this issue now?

"What do I have to do to fix this?"

"Let me make love to you. No tricks. No games. And I'll give you your home back with one simple signature on the documents in my hand."

"Never. I'm getting a lawyer."

Isaiah passed the papers to Tye, "Then good luck losing a fight that can't be won."

Isaiah left the home and immediately Tye started to panic. He sat down and read the documents Isaiah had handed over to him. Based on the documents, the church now owned the home. He contacted a lawyer friend of Herbert that the man had planned on consulting with during the point when he thought he could actually win the campaign and become the mayor of Riverbed.

Tye scanned the documents via his phone and sent it over to the lawyer along with the details of the situation. Instead of getting the answers that he wanted as soon as possible, Tye was informed he would have to wait. Tye spent the entire day doing his own research and not finding many direct answers. Chaz arrived home and joined Tye in his bedroom.

Chaz crashed onto the bed, "I love what I do. But I hate doing it."

"Long day?"

"Very," Chaz said, "It was educational but stressful. How about you?"

"The church owns the house," Isaiah said, "The same house I promised my father that I would take care of."

"How is this even possible?"

"Because Glenda is the moral police. And this is the house of sin. We're one of her many targets in town."

"What are you going to do?" Chaz asked.

"A lawyer friend of my father is looking into everything," Tye said, "All I can do is wait and stress."

Chaz crawled over to Tye and kissed him, "We both can't be stressed. Breathe in, breathe out, relax."

Chaz kissed Tye as they stripped naked. Tye slowly moved his head downward toward Chaz's bulging dick. He shut his eyes and slipped Chaz's dick into his mouth. Chaz started groaning as Tye sucked his dick. Chaz put his hand on the back of Tye's head and forced him to go down deeper onto his dick. They switched positions and Chaz started to suck Tye's dick. Done swapping head, they turned things up.

Tye turned over and arched his booty in the air. Chaz dove in tongue first. Tye found himself moaning and enjoying Chaz's tongue deep in him. Chaz tongued Tye down into submission before he started to slip his dick into him. At the moment, Tye felt no stress just pleasure. Chaz stroked into Tye rough and didn't ease up at any point. Tye wanted Chaz to pound him harder.

"Harder," Tye demanded.

Chaz went in harder. Tye was surprised Chaz had so much energy in him after a long day at the hospital. But he knew all of this was coming from Chaz's heart. Chaz was going above and beyond to calm him after a stressful day even though his was just as bad. Tye would never let Isaiah touch him, not even to save this home. The only touch he needed was Chaz's.

Chaz started to bust in Tye, "Fuck."

Chaz kept stroking his dick into Tye until it went soft. They both remained in bed making out.

"I will win," Tye said as he held onto Chaz.

"I know," Chaz said, "The lawyer will come through and you will win."

But those words didn't matter. Because two days later Tye received a text from the lawyer explaining that all of those moves Glenda made were legal. Tye didn't know why he expected an easy victory. The elite of Riverbed rarely loss. He knew for sure that he wasn't going to go running to Isaiah for help. Tye would have to do something that was rarely done in Riverbed, tell the naked truth.

The time for saving face was done. His reputation was already deep in the ditch. It was time for him to show the people of Riverbed that this was not a house of sin. But instead the home he was raised in and where his father changed the lives of his many clients. And Tye would do this at the biggest event this week in Riverbed, Isaiah's first sermon.

On Sunday morning, Tye sat outside of Rivers Baptist Church with the documents in his hand that Isaiah had given to him. All he needed was his signature.

"Are you sure you want to do this alone?" Chaz asked.

"I can handle them," Tye said, "All of them."

Chaz kissed Tye, "I love you. You know that, right?"

Tye smirked at him, "I love you too."

"Are we together?" Chaz questioned, "Because I want to be together."

"We're together," Tye said, "And we will be together in my father's home."

Tye got out of the car with his heart racing. All of a sudden it felt extremely hot outside and his mouth was dry. But today needed to happen. This was the only chance he had at keeping his promise to his father to take care of his house.

Tye entered the quiet church as Isaiah was in the middle of his sermon. Isaiah stopped speaking and looked down the center aisle as Tye walked with all eyes on him. A few of the faces in the pews seemed to be welcoming him while others clearly didn't want him here this morning. Isaiah's mother Glenda was one of those people who wanted Tye escorted out of the church based on the eye roll she delivered as he reached the front of the center aisle.

Isaiah stood looking nervous behind the podium that was marked with a crucifix, "What are you doing?"

Tye held the documents up in his hand, "I need you to sign these papers and give me my father's house back. That is all I want from you...nothing else." Tye started to shed tears, "I made a promise to my father and if I lose this house I will break it. It's clear this is an issue that I can't solve by scheming and lying. I know that's how things work in this town but this morning I'm not playing by those rules. Isaiah, sign these documents right now. I'm not leaving until you do. I'll stand here all day until you do so."

Isaiah looked from Tye to his mother, "Um..."

"Do it, please," Tye said, "I'm begging you. And I'm not ashamed to admit that."

"Tye..." Isaiah uttered.

Tye took a step toward the podium with the documents held out and tears running down his face, "Please."

The church members sat in silence as everybody awaited a response from Isaiah.

Isaiah stepped from behind the podium and approached Tye, "Why do this here?"

"Because I want everybody in this church to see that you are a good man," Tye said, "A forgiving one who will not judge me because of my past, my present, or my future mistakes. A man who will change the way things are done in this town." He lowered his voiced and whispered, "And a man who basically raped me but will get away with it no matter what I say. But can receive my forgiveness right here in his own church and have that night never brought up again if he just sign these fucking papers."

Tye used up all of his options. He gave a speech, shed some tears, and begged. All Tye had now was the hope that Isaiah was harboring some guilt about the night he and Chef Bam tricked him into an unconsented threesome.

Isaiah took the documents from Tye's hands, "Fine."

"Lord no," A puzzled Glenda stressed from her seat, "Isaiah, child, what are you doing?"

Tye passed Isaiah a pen. Isaiah signed the documents and handed them back to Tye.

Tye turned away from Isaiah wearing a big grin while most in the pews looked disgusted with both of them.

"I won," Tye declared.

Tye folded up the documents, dried the tears from his face, and made his way toward the exit of the church. He came to church this morning armed with his emotions, desperation, and the threat of the naked truth as a weapon. And most importantly, Tye kept his promise to his father.

Naked
www.tysonanthony.com
Thank You

59634825R00111

Made in the USA
Charleston, SC
10 August 2016